ADAM JORDAN

No Man's World

Book I - Imposition

First edition

Editing by Courtney Andersson
Cover art by Jeff Brown Graphics

This book was professionally typeset on Reedsy.
Find out more at reedsy.com

Contents

Chapter 00 – Prologue

An unworldly being and his blood prodigy stared out through a glasslike bubble at a strange planet. The father and son had shared many moments together in the command quarters talking about the vastness of space and the possibilities of a new home. This time, the mood was grounded and dismissive. In an ungodly tongue, the two cosmic foreigners discussed their pressing familial matters.

"This ship is suffocating me. The endless halls and the oppressive chambers . . . we are caged like creatures lost. I want to see colored skies." The young one had deserted his manners, unable to deny his deepening frustration.

The father listened, but kept his gaze upon the peculiar world visible through the ship's viewport from the safety of their stranded star fleet. The bustling Vagantem lab technicians and engineers worked tirelessly behind them; some in large mechanized suits of metal and rubber, others in gleaming stardust coats that fluttered against their bone-stretched skin and hunched spines. They worked with great machinery of tools and wire attached to the distant ceiling of the ship; hands of the dark god, or so they were called.

"What could you possibly know about the skies of worlds? Have the sons of soldiers and pilots painted pictures in your dreams?"

the patriarch chastised with subtle scorn. The Vagantem boy remained silent, though the tentacled arms of his lips twitched irritably. *"Skies are nothing but blankets, meant for younglings and dreamers. The black of space is the celestial banner of truth, and you must know it deeply. You are a youngling no more, and I will not endure your whining; I do not have the patience your mother once blessed me with."* The father's words stung like the crack of a whip.

The son turned to face him, clutching tears back before they could be discovered. *"I should not have made this about me, Father. I beg your forgiveness,"* he said reluctantly. The father responded with a staunch silence and the stillness of a statue, which felt almost as if it were an attempt to ignore and forget the interaction that had just occurred. His attention returned to the viewport. The father donned not a stardust coat, like his son and some of the others wore, but rather a commanding twilight robe that was one with his shadow. It was embroidered with symbols and metals, both ancient and new, and lined with a pale translucent edging.

". . . Our people," the boy said at last, *". . . deserve better. This is no life for the Vagantem."* As he spoke, he wore a stern mask that kept secret his weeping soul.

"This is exactly the life we deserve," the father replied, ushering surprise and hopelessness into his son. The father could feel the bewildered black and grey eyes of the young one set upon him. Without lifting his gaze from the mostly blue rock, he continued, *"Our home was not lost, but erased. We are not refugees, but self-imposed exiles. This will be our life, and the lives of future generations . . . all because we couldn't protect it. Because we couldn't see what was happening."* The father held his thinning shoulders proudly, but a weary sorrow crept into his tone.

The son had yet to recognize this emerging new state of the strong and caring figure he once knew and loved, though he understood that the recent loss of his mother was a festering wound in his father's heart.

"I still do not understand why we can't make this our new home," the son gestured with the nautilus-like tendrils of his face toward the rotating globe below them.

The father's tendrils coiled up in disdain. *"This hellscape is tainted by the blood and ambition of a broken people. A sad joke, carried out by our great and wise leader,"* he winced with the iron press of contempt. *"No . . . this will never be our home."*

The son looked up and felt an unfamiliar sadness. Not as painful as the death of his mother, but an itchy and seething sting that would inevitably grow numb, yet forever remain. His father had once been a bright light, joyous and proud. He was the top executive of the Observant Fleet's Engineering Core and had inspired many minds, young and old. Over the troubled years he had devolved into a brooding and agitated shadow that gloomed over his work and numbed his days with synthetic drugs and poisoned fragrances.

"Then why are we here?" the heir asked, disregarding the formal tone he was expected to keep.

The father began to look worried and unsure, and did not reprimand his son for the discourtesy in his voice. *"They have a role to play in all of this,"* he replied softly.

"Like the Critori?" the youth pressed.

The father, however, did not answer, likely revisiting the horrors of his memories and talking to ghosts within his oval head. He seemed increasingly gaunt as he continued to stare at the once vibrant greens and blues of Earth, now faded and murky. Through dark clouds, a massive structure fixed on

3

the western continent flickered with reflected beams of light dancing off the peculiar surface. Other structures, few in number and smaller in scale, were stationed throughout the limited landmasses on the planet's surface.

Chapter I – Ghosts and Vermin

The sun seemed long dead and the darkness ran heavy, but Shane the restless remained vigilant, watching over his fellow survivors. He was a quiet man; tall, slender, and awake, with ebony iron skin. The group was settled in a decrepit hotel parking garage that had vines and roots breaking free from their old-world restraints. Though nature was reclaiming what was once hers, the ancient destruction was still apparent and still haunting. Shane watched the fire, losing himself in the laughing flames, until he heard subtle slashes and cracks, and then the squish of soaked flesh. He looked over and noticed one of his sleeping companions was twitching faintly.

"Gus!" The rest of the group started to rouse and wake while Shane ran to Gus's seemingly possessed corpse. "Gus!" he yelled again as he grabbed him. The dying man's stomach was dancing and jumping as if something alive was inside. Shane lifted his bloodied shirt, which revealed a tunnel into the man's stomach. Ringed tails of pink flesh and orange filth whirled around outside the festering intrusion. A monstrous rat, like a demon the size of a house cat, crawled out of the corpse defensively, eyed Shane, and hissed. The smell made the survivors dizzy as they rushed to grab their limited gear and supplies and escape the horde that was soon to follow. They made for the streets and left the underworld—and Gus—for the rats to rule.

They made it aboveground just as the sun was birthed into the sky, and they stared out over the carnage of the old world, stubbornly resistant to the beauty of the new. They said nothing in remembrance of their fallen friend, not even a shared thought or feeling, and instead simply kept on. The group was hungry; it was time to hunt and scavenge.

They all moved to a bus parked outside, reinforced with metal plates and defended with spears. It had *"The Magic School Bus"* painted on the side in dark crimson paint—or blood. Carli, a young, beautiful, and pale ghost of a woman stepped in to store some of the bigger luggage. A pistol she had carried from the start of it all radiated with pride through its holster, despite the top layer of soot and rust. Claimed with a single bullet left in the chamber, it had never been used, but it had become an extension of her all the same over the years. Coldblood they called her from time to time, Carli the coldblood. The remaining two of the four-person group were Leonard the loud and Bastian the enlightened. Leonard was an angry, explosive, and dangerous dwarf with a coat of tattoos while Bastian was a giant beast of a man with a friendly touch and a soft, low voice. They separated into two groups—Shane with Carli and Bastian with Leonard—to hunt and scavenge the city ruins they had called home for the last few days.

"We've been here too long, man; I'm fucking sick of eating rats and roaches. I want some real fuckin' meat," Leonard spat with exhausted rage. "There isn't any gas or whatever the fuck else he wants out here, or anywhere else in this godforsaken ruin, let alone this world. The bus is a lost cause, and this is a waste of time."

Bastian listened until Leonard's complaints were interrupted by a low baritone full of hatred and fear. The two men froze, and from behind the crooked frame of what once was a car, a healthy grizzly bear cub emerged. Trailing close with maternal instinct, its ten-foot monstrous mother also appeared. The mother tried to shrug off her weakness, but the radioactive creature could barely stand on her wobbling legs. Its fur had mostly fallen off, it was missing an eye, and part of the skull was visible. The bear stood high on its hind legs briefly in an attempt to drown them in shadow, but it could not bear its own weight and soon came crashing down on all fours. The bear continued to try in vain to scare the two intruders away with tired growls, knowing it was too weak to put up a fight.

"You got this, Bastian." Leonard nudged the giant.

"You have the mallet?" he inquired. Leonard handed him a large rusted wrench from his belt. Bastian approached the dying mother, who started to head his way, growing fiercer with every step. The large man wound up and chucked the wrench directly at the beast as soon as it started its charge. The wrench broke through the bear's weakened skull and it fell to its face, burying its nose in the ground. The momentum carried the corpse and it slid in the dust, lifeless. Leonard whooped and giddied as he ran up to inspect the fallen creature while Bastian lost himself in the dead mother's gaze. He was destroyed inside evermore.

"Where's the baby?" the smaller man blustered. Bastian stayed still and quiet while he listened to Leonard catch up to the offspring and kill the squealing innocence. Suddenly, large winged shadows began to circle around them, and fear grasped hold once again. Leonard stared up at the sky in awe as the cub lay bleeding beside him. Bastian ran up and grabbed the dead whelp by the foot, and they both fled the scene while the incoming screeches blasted painfully louder. A gargoyle with no eyes or even sockets landed on the lifeless rot of the mother bear, drooling over its latest meal. The flying creature had a short swine snout and its teeth glistened like butcher's blades. It spread its three-meter wingspan gloriously, like a shadow king, and signaled its harem of mates to the feast.

At a safe distance, they slowed down and caught their breaths. "Let's start heading back . . . need to prep the cub before dark," Bastian wheezed.

* * *

"I think it's time to leave," Shane said reluctantly.

Carli looked at him, confused, as they continued to walk. "You say that like it's a bad thing . . . like you'd rather stay," she eventually let out.

"I feel a little safer here, and I'm tired," he said.

"We're all tired, Shane," she replied.

"I know. We can't keep running and hiding. We need a home, even if it is temporary; we need to hold on to something as long as we can," he finished.

"That'd be nice," Carli scoffed.

"This old city felt right for a moment, but there is nothing here but ghosts and vermin. Tonight will be our last here. We'll have to leave the bus, take as much as we can, and hope for a good hunt," Shane said while staring off into the rubble and fallen infrastructure; dead relics and ruined monuments to mankind.

"Then let's find a secluded spot while we still have walls and doors." She grabbed him by the butt. Shane didn't flinch, but was unaffected by it. "Let's fuck." She got closer and he put a

8

heavy hand on her shoulder.

"Not now, Carli."

"So . . . you just never wanna fuck me again?" she barked resentfully.

"Stop!" he yelled. They both stopped and faced each other, then with fervent whispers, ignored the world around them and spoke of secrets past.

They both returned to find Leonard feeding a fire and Bastian skinning their dinner. "How'd you find this poor little guy?" Carli smiled in disbelief.

"Luck," Bastian said with a smile and a hint of remorse. He drew his arms out of the carcass, slick and red up to the elbow, ridding the animal of its entrails and nuisances. The night was coming, but daylight was still mostly about; a cooking fire could be seen from a distance. The cub meat was tender and sweet, far better than venison, and with a deeper red than beef. The feast felt almost gluttonous with their shrunken stomachs.

Carli wandered off to use the ladies' room and squatted over some dirt and cracked asphalt. The sound of water pressure and the soggy slurp of the ground filled the air, followed by half a footstep. The figure was attempting, and failing, to be inconspicuous. "What the fuck do you want? I'm pissing!" Carli barked as Leonard revealed himself from the shadows.

"Why you gotta be so ruthless with me, girl?" he replied with an obnoxious grin.

"Did I invite you to come over and pee with me?" Carli asked rhetorically and kept on peeing, unphased until she finished and stood up, unashamed as she buckled her belt and adjusted her holster.

"Look, we used to be close, and I could make you laugh any time; you were always smiling, for the most part, until you started fucking him."

She looked at him, surprise, irritation, and tiredness on her face.

"Yeaaahh, we know, fuck I think even Gus knew," he said hotheadedly.

"Are you jealous?" she asked coyly.

"I don't care, I'm just waiting for my tur—" before he finished, Carli delivered a fist of female fury so hard to the dwarf's nose that he was lifted into the air before abruptly landing on his back and losing the wind in his chest. She walked away while the dwarf coughed and desperately tried to catch his breath. The noise of the man's desperate recovery faded in the backdrop.

She saw the flame in the distance and realized that she'd taken a considerably long stroll from the camp spot. She then grew irritated at the sight. The last light of dusk had fallen, and surely there was nothing else to cook. *Why haven't they put it out yet?* As she finally got close, she heard nothing but the crackling and chewing of the fire, which she found even more odd. She took out her gun and had it ready as she walked slowly toward the silence. When she approached, she saw Shane and Bastian kneeling with their hands tied behind their backs and mouths gagged with stained rags. Before she could react, a knife was at her throat, tracing the crease in her neck. A heavy breath and sour stench boomed against her ear, followed by a frothy mixture of spit and sweat dripping onto her shoulder.

"Put the piece down, sweetie," a voice whispered into her ear. Another figure quickly grabbed the pistol out of her hands, and she was thrown down to the floor with her comrades.

The fire revealed the demons' faces. Three men, all on the verge of starvation with their whole skeletal systems on display. Each of them had pieces of themselves carved out from their legs and arms and other meat and fat reservoirs.

The sight of their new prisoners clearly delighted them; they looked like sick children seeing candy for the first time. One was tall and lumbering, an albino completely hairless without even an eyebrow to keep his shriveled skin warm. Another was subhuman. It was blind and lacked pupils; its eyes were pure white windows into its black soul. It acted like a feral animal that had lost its ability to talk long ago, growling and laughing like a hyena. The third member and ringleader of the trio was a drooling ghost of a man. He had a sable skin tone and wore nothing but tattered pants, and his feet were bloodied and callused. He held a large metal pole with an ugly shard of glass tied securely at the tip and carried a rusty switchblade in the other hand. The feral one was bleeding profusely, but none seemed to worry. After another moment, the ringleader began to speak.

"Are we too late for dinner?" The feral one began to yelp and mutter while the ringleader continued, "Where on Earth did you find this?" He pointed to the fur and bones piled on the ground. Shane, Bastian, and Carli all kept still and silent, each contemplating possible escape opportunities while the white hairless one kept his evil eyes on Carli.

"You guys look tough . . . and fed." The leader smiled at them and made eye contact with each. "We haven't seen people in a long . . . long time, but I always knew there were still some out here, souls denied the beyond. You remind me of the days of the old world, full of faces and names. You know . . . I stood right there in front of that liquor store every single day, begging for scraps. I would sleep there too, because the guy who ran the store liked me; he believed in me." As he spoke, he was no longer looking at his captives, but rather at the living

11

and bustling city as it once was; a dreamy veil inside his head.

"I would tell people to turn to the Lord and escape the inevitable. With all that I have done I will not be welcomed into the gates of the afterlife, and I wanted no one to suffer my fate. So, I realized my role in the universe. I am here to shepherd the lost and guide them in the raptured land." The feral one moaned and cried. "Settle, my brother. They will first understand . . . and then, we will feast."

The feral creature ignored his words, as if he could no longer understand them. Suddenly, he bit into his own arm at the limited space he hadn't consumed already. He ripped out a mouthful of foul flesh and began to eat it without pain or hesitation. Black and green juices squirted from his putrid mastication. Bastian and Carli were astounded and frightened to a level they had not experienced in some time, and the noxious mixture of sound and sight made them all feel grimly ill.

Shane began to mutter desperately through his gag, his words indistinct. He started to sweat as the leader approached and kneeled to face him.

"Your squealing and suffering will end soon, and you will be able to move on from this world. When the angels came to take the chosen, they raised hell from the inferno and left the undecided here to be tested, for it is up to the soul to redeem itself, and you all have. We are the gatekeepers. You will feed me and my brothers with your flesh, and we will send you to the stars where—" Before he could finish his speech, the feral one dropped to the ground and began to seize intensely until his life force escaped through his last dying yelp. The other two turned toward the mangled sycophant and stared at his rotten corpse for a moment. "He has moved on . . . at last," the leader whispered to himself.

The moment proved long enough for Shane to pull the gag out of his mouth with the use of his shoulder. He coughed to clear his throat and spat out lingering fibers, dirt, and mucus before speaking. "They weren't angels, they weren't demons, and they weren't human. They saw our world and they wanted it, and we destroyed it so they couldn't have it. They contained the destruction, reshaped the land, and then they got bored and left. But this is still Earth, the dark winter is over, and we are still human. Come with us and leave this graveyard. The forests are full of fruit and game to hunt—there is a whole new world outside of this."

The two remaining cannibals faced Shane with hungry grins. "Then why are you here?" the leader asked, accusation clear in his voice.

"I'm glad your bellies are full . . . and now there's less to share," the pale one said before starting to creep toward Carli. "I am going to boil your eyeballs, fry your brains, and spit roast the rest, but you, gorgeous . . . you I am going to eat raw and bloody."

A whistle and a hum grew louder until a piece of rubble cracked into the albino's skull from behind. His face broke the ground as they collided. The leader scrambled for the gun the now unconscious oaf had dropped. Once he recovered the loaded firearm, he looked up in time to see the rush of a leaping dwarf.

Leonard lunged off the top of the broken-down bus with a jagged machete in hand. He slashed the chief cannibal's face, but not before the fatal flash of fire and metal. They both tumbled and rolled to the ground. Smoke followed shortly after. The lacerated ghost failed to see through the crimson creek streaming down his face. He tried to stand, but Leonard hacked at the sinews behind his knees and the demon was demobilized.

After a lazy sigh and gust of release, he spoke his dying words. ". . . I will never escape this world . . . I am bound to the gates of judgment." The demon resembled a fearful and sorrowful man, and everything he once was escaped through a final tear. He wasn't afraid of Leonard, but of the tormenting eternity that awaited.

Leonard allowed the unconscious ghost to breathe his final breaths and looked down to see that he was standing in a blackened puddle of his own blood, thicker than water. "Eat steel, rat." He finished the ghost with a chop to the cranium; the blade stuck in bone and had to be pried free. The ghost died in silence.

Carli freed the others while Leonard struggled, holding together his blown-apart stomach. His hands were sticky and his vision blurred. Carli made her way over to the albino cannibal lying face-first in the ground and stomped his skull in with her boot.

Bastian looked at Shane and muttered, "You cannot reason with animals." Shane, looking into the distance, nodded absently.

"Take me with you guys, I wanna see the wilderness one more time. I'll make it." Leonard's breaths were getting coarse and his lungs were filling with blood. The scarlet ooze surged past the closed corners of his chapped lips. His leaking stomach acids were eating the surrounding organs and corroding the protective linings within. He was tough in spirit, but that could only get one so far.

The group started their trek out of the dead city. Carli tried to grab Leonard's arm to help him, but he pushed her away with the limited strength he could muster. "I don't need anything! I never . . . needed anything. If I can't make it, then I don't deserve . . . get there." They had never seen a man trying so hard to speak, words forced out like a kidney stone for every syllable. For a long time, they all knew something to be true: despite all the promises of hope, fate rarely put aside its cruelty.

They walked through the night and left the fire to die out on its own. The sun started to breach the sky again, burdening them with its blinding light. They were all exhausted and dehydrated, and then Leonard began to give out. He tripped on the small bones of buildings and broken streets, then lay on the vengeful ground, motionless. His trail of blood ended. The group stopped to face their dying comrade in respect and admiration for all of who he was. They were not used to having the chance to say goodbye.

"Fuck it . . . this . . . good spot." He could barely get the words out. Carli went to kneel by his side. "Go . . . let . . . let . . . me die . . . thank . . ." Then a breeze filtered by and extinguished his flame.

Bastian looked at his fallen friend, at the certainty of death. The soft brute's soul recoiled, almost wishing it had been his life. With a sigh, he picked the corpse up and swung it over his shoulder, dripping. "We'll bury him outside," he said, and they kept on.

Chapter II – Cliff and the Boys

The rats followed the chain of blood that led them to the fleeing group, but were restricted to the shadows, for the sun would burn their eyes and minds. On the horizon, dead old-world trees rested in their coats of permanent ash and clinker. Past the border of scorched bark, though, were massive trees the size of redwoods with thick yellow leaves, white bark, and blood orange vines hanging down like ribbons in the wind. The giants were spaced out from each other, allowing an assortment of saplings, oaks, and other unrecognizable trees and shrubbery to form in between.

The variety of trees stood above rocks consumed with maroon algae and pink mushrooms. Vibrantly colored flowers and berries also decorated the alien undergrowth. The forest was loud; the soundwaves of unknowable creatures collided with each other and ricocheted off the magnificent guardian trees. Far off were great crowning peaks, sharp and jagged as crude blades. The group welcomed the sight of the beautiful new land that did not resemble Earth. They had entered the vast city from the southeasternmost part and now exited through the north. The lands they had traversed so far had been vastly different biomes, and now, they came across yet another lost world. The rats retreated and kept to the ruins. The sun was setting, and another day began to end. While Bastian started to dig a final resting spot for Leonard, Carli gathered berries and wood for a quick boil and Shane went off to conduct a basic perimeter patrol.

Shane's patrols were becoming obsessive and paranoid, and he circled the perimeter in a half mile radius ten times. On his eleventh, he took his time. Finally, Bastian and Carli grew impatient, stopped waiting, and buried Leonard in the planet. They both lacked words, again lost in silence.

"Do you feel anything?" Carli eventually let out.

"I would have given my life for his . . . and instead, he gave his for us. It was going to happen one way or another. I feel hunger, thirst, exhaustion, even fear, but there isn't any room to feel anything else. We've lost ourselves, and we are no better than any creature out here." Bastian hung his head and dwelled deep in thought.

"We've never been," she replied. "We're even worse a lot of the time."

Leonard's face crept into Shane's thoughts as he walked, and he tried to push it from his mind. The face looked at him coolly, and he shook his head in disgust before cutting the memory out in anger and frustration. He eventually decided his persistent circling had gone on too long, and came back to camp still shouldering the weight of uncertainty. "I'll take first watch; you guys should try to get some sleep," he said.

"You sure you're not going to wander off and leave us to get eaten by a giant snake or something in our sleep?" Carli said with civil sarcasm, though Shane took it as if she were genuinely scared. Humor was usually lost on him, and his ignorance warmed her stone heart at times.

"I would never leave watch," he said, concerned she did not

17

trust him.

"Okay, good. Night." Carli left it on a sweet note, and she and Bastian quickly fell into dreams of loss and hunger.

Shane quickly put to rest the already dying fire after his pot of water from a nearby brook came to a boil. The night ran particularly bright this evening. Caught in orbit and relatively closer to the planet than on most nights, a plump and confident moon seemed to rest in place. It emanated a new violet shade, and with no contesting light it was the centerpiece in the darkness; god's watchful eye. Large, unrecognizable insects flew through the moon's purple radiance, and their wings echoed in the hush of a sleepy night. For a moment, Shane found peace in the world, but the feeling slowly drained away, and he endured a strange, overwhelming anxiety. A flock of birds scared from their roosts resembled a black cloud moving fast against a starry sky. Suddenly, the bushes began to dance in the distance. He immediately stood and grabbed the gruesome blade he'd inherited from Leonard.

"Guys!" he said as loud as he could while still remaining within the definition of a whisper. The two were deep in sleep, and he couldn't wake them. It seemed to him that a vacuum of silence had dropped over them like a noiseless atom bomb. Nothing was heard until the brush ruffled slightly behind the vigilant protector. He turned around and approached, ready to defend himself or go on the offensive. Shane kicked a bush, hoping to scare whatever it was out of hiding. As soon as he did, a growl and a hiss emanated from the dark. His fear began to ease.

He kicked the bush a second time and was immediately met with a snarling blur, only for the mammal to stop roughly twenty feet from him. The creature was no bigger than a fox but resembled a weasel with a striped black and brown coat. It had a trail of long hairs that ran down its spine and a pair of sabertooth fangs displayed outside its jaws. It was a creature of many worlds ago, resurrected by off-world science. It looked at Shane, scared and curious, frozen by the combination of the two. Shane slowly reached for a rock resting on the ground by the dead fire, hoping to ensure protein for tomorrow's breakfast.

Then the entire universe was interrupted by a powerful roar that lasted for a few terrifying moments. The bellow blew Shane to the ground, and his prey was gone in an instant. Bastian and Carli immediately woke and sprung into protocol, panicking on the verge of defecation. They each grabbed a weapon and moved into a defensive formation, backs to each other. Carli reached for her now empty holster and bit her lip to a bleed at the sudden realization. They stayed in that exact position throughout the entirety of the night, going through each hour without rest or relief. When the sun eventually came up, the sleep deprivation began to poison them with weakness. Still, the years on the road had hardened them; they would remain on constant alert for as long as needed.

"We should move," Carli said.

"No, it either knows we are here or it's still close," Shane responded.

"How do you know that?" she asked.

"Guys!" Bastian interrupted. They both shut up and looked to him. "Listen." In the distance, it started off as an ominous hum that turned into the ugly purr of an engine. Before they could react, powerful paws began to rhythmically slap the earth as a monster galloped toward them. It was a beast the size of a horse and it carried a shell on its back that sprouted large, protruding spikes. The creature's tail was vastly longer than its body and had a whiplike end coiled at the tip, its hind legs were slightly longer than its front, and it brandished the face of a dragon.

Shane and Carli turned and frantically ran in the opposite direction. Bastian chucked the large wrench he'd christened "the mallet" before he turned to do the same. The wrench went over the reptile's head and chipped a curved spike on its shell. The creature was unfazed and ever ferocious as it hurtled toward them.

Bastian tripped, and Shane immediately turned around to pull him up and shove him with all his might in the direction Carli was headed. He knew running was futile; the monster was at his shadow. Shane faced the beast before it pounced on him. Instinctively, he raised his left arm in defense, and the dragon latched onto it, teeth clasping around his elbow. They slammed into the earth with the animal pressing on the man's chest, almost caving in his heart and soul. The creature swung its head back and forth until the razor-sharp jaws sliced through Shane; bone, flesh, and cloth alike were rent until the last sinews stretched to their limit and snapped like rubber bands. The dragon triumphantly looked up toward the sky and swallowed the arm whole. At the edge of consciousness, Shane hoped that they were far away by now, but Bastian was not. He remained, in shock and horrified, frozen by indecision.

Suddenly, engines busted the foray and an AR-15 sprayed the carapace and hind legs of the animal, miraculously missing Shane. The first truck zipped past while another skidded through the mud to a dramatic halt. The creature turned to face its opponents but endured a shower of lead, this time to the face. For a moment, it seemed resilient to the bombardment, but it eventually fell, shaking the ground with its dead drop.

A group of four exited the truck after the kill was made, barrels raised. Bastian lifted his massive arms, palms open in surrender. There was a small-boned young man holding a gun too big for him, a grim man with empty eyes, a fiery man with nothing but aimless vengeance in his heart, and the last, presumably the leader, was a man that matched Bastian in stature. He had a boisterous red beard with grey spots and a short military haircut that accompanied his torn and shabby uniform.

"You're a big fuckin' fella aren't ya?" he bellowed. The initial truck returned with three additional men and a hostage Carli. She was bound and gagged by duct tape, with her nose barely able to grasp the humid air. Smoke and mist crept by. The three bandits were wickedly riled and all had a military style similar to the leader. The red captain looked at Carli with crass delight, towering over all except Bastian. "The spoils of war are good, my friends." He licked his lips while his eyes swelled.

"Don't fucking touch her!" Bastian roared, frightening several of the men with exception of the leader and the empty-eyed one.

"Too fucking late, buddy! I like your size; you could be of some goddamn value to us, but you got to let her go, and you got to do it fast. She'll only slow you down . . . trust me," the leader explained while Bastian expressed rage in every fiber of his being. His bronze skin blushed and thick veins of boiling blue surfaced on his face. His breathing quickened. The leader cocked his head and lifted his thick red brow like an arching caterpillar, subtly hinting that Bastian should calm down. He did not. "So, it's gonna be the hard way, huh?" the red man finally let out, giving him ample opportunity to comply.

"Let's jus' fill 'em up with lead, Cliff," the fiery man spat.

"Nope, that's too good for this sack of shit," Cliff insisted. "Why don't you boys have a good ol' fashion beatdown? Here . . . teach him, blood him." The captain chuckled as he shoved the small-boned youth toward the cackling trio.

"Pathetic coward!" Bastian yelled, the exertion making him feel light-headed. The fiery man went to swing, but Bastian's stone face absorbed it. He answered with even more force, and his brick of a fist was a gale of wind to his opponent's flame. As one of their own fell unconscious, the men holding Carli dropped her, and the entire gang began to mercilessly beat on her friend with the ends of their guns and bootheels. Bastian fought back valiantly, but he could not block all the strikes, and each exacted their toll on his body until his ribs were cracked and face was pummeled.

Cliff let his boys continue their work while he dragged the unconscious one away; the once raucous inferno of a man dwindled down to a mere cinder. He lifted and tossed the man into the bed of the pickup.

"Alright boys, whoever is gonna take turns with the girl has to take the turtle back with them. Anyone else, we're moving out." Before the young one could understand, Cliff hopped in his truck and drove off.

Three of the bandits began to rip Carli's clothes off while impatiently tripping over their own dropping pants. Carli was able to kick one of them in the face with her steel toe, and his nose began to leak copiously, streaking his skin like spilled wine.

"You fucking cunt!" He punched her in the face and she was rendered unconscious; seemingly lifeless, and then all three of them had their way with her . . . penetrating her . . .

bickering and fighting each other over who was next and how long they got to have with her flesh. The grim man with the empty eyes turned away, listening to them but refusing to look. He ransacked their scattered supplies and grabbed the only thing of note, Leonard's gleaming blade. He found their stash of spoiling food cans, some crushed and trampled, others still viable. He took only one, leaving the rest for his comrades, if they weren't too horny to look about. The defilers only had twenty minutes in them, and now it was the young blood's turn. The boy was awkward and unsure, thrusting in and out until the surrounding laughter discouraged him from concluding. They decided to take her back to base for future use. They threw her naked, comatose body in the backseat.

Bastian began to show limited signs of life, but only the grim one noticed. He stared, and his empty eyes now looked curious as well as hollow. With much effort, the highwaymen dragged the dead dragon up the trunk ramp. Its carcass barely fit, and its head hung over on one side while its tail dragged through the dust on the other. "You guys leave without me . . . I'm headed to the West Post," the grim man muttered. The driver scoffed and drove off unconcerned; the weight of the beast slowing the vehicle. After he ensured they were out of sight, the grim man walked up to Bastian and pressed a Glock to his temple, racking the slide and cocking the striker.

"Not yet . . . I'm not ready," Bastian whispered.

"Let me put you to rest, brother," the grim man said.

"I need more time," Bastian coughed out.

"There is no time . . . you need peace, my friend. I can give you that."

". . . Let me die on my own." Bastian slowly caught his breath. The merciful man looked at him with both intrigue and

23

remorse before leaving. Bastian watched the man vanish, then looked over to Shane, mangled and forgotten.

Chapter III – The Reckoning

Bastian crawled through the yellow grass and found that Shane had, before passing out, helped stave off the flow of blood from his open wound by using a ripped piece of his shirt as a tourniquet. Bastian looked over at their trampled camp and targeted an empty pot, relatively clean from the last boil. He tried to stand but collapsed after one step and began to have trouble breathing. He crawled to the pot on a long, agonizing journey on all fours, then had to repeat the grueling distance back to Shane. On his way, he grabbed dry grass and sticks, eventually acquiring a considerable collection.

Shane was lying in a spot of shade, but just ten feet from him was a powerful beam of sunlight that won its way through the giant canopy and bleached the earth. Bastian formed a tinder nest with the dry grass and twigs and placed it directly in the center of the ray. He then took a fractured eyeglass from his pocket, wiped the soot off with his dirty shirt, and held the lens so as to focus the sun's power onto the nest. Eventually it started to smoke, and a small fire was born. He babied the flame, covering it from the wrong breeze but giving it air to breathe.

Slowly, he began to fuel it from his pile of larger scions and let it bloom into an orange flower. He then held the pot over the flame, just high enough for it to lick the metal for several searing moments until the bottom glowed red. Bastian crawled the last ten feet toward Shane; when he reached him, he ripped off the makeshift tourniquet, spurting a red mist. He then proceeded to grab what was left of Shane's limb and pressed it against the scalding iron to cauterize it. Shane woke up, back from the dead and yelling violently, but Bastian refused to let go until he thought the flesh was sufficiently singed. He eventually released and allowed Shane space to scream and squirm in uncertain agony.

An unaccounted for amount of time slipped by as they lay in the same spot around a fire that was barely kept alive. Daylight diminished and the night fell heavy. Both of them sat there, defeated and crippled with nothing to listen to but the snapping wood and whispering flame. Despite the dark and danger, they let it burn out on its own; their minds were elsewhere. Bastian handed a dented canteen of water to his friend after he had already taken a sip, and Shane grabbed it with the only functional arm he had left.

"We are going to find her," Shane said firmly.

"And we are going to kill every single one of them," Bastian finished. He looked to Shane, who nodded.

* * *

Carli woke up frail and beaten; when her eyes opened, she could only see white. She began to cry, and she realized she couldn't hear anything, not even her own sobs. Before she started to panic, a warm, delicate hand took hold of hers. The hand, though friendly, scared her even more when she realized she was restrained, unable to move. She began to struggle and scream, and the sound of her voice slowly started to penetrate her consciousness. The blank whiteness became lights, and then a white room with medical gear and supplies. Carli felt a comfort she did not recognize, a heavenly voice that dripped down her ears like honey.

"Shhhh, my dear. There is nothing trying to harm you at the moment." A beautiful and plump woman with long wavy red hair that fell like molten lava over her shoulders smiled at her. Carli looked at her in awe and hope. "I took the tape off you 'cuz it looked hard to breathe—you're not gonna make me regret that, are you?" Carli shook her head in response. "Good. I also put some clothes on you, but they're mine, so they'd probably fall right off if you stood. We'll fetch you another outfit soon. That's another thing, you probably already feel this, but those boys were pretty rough on you, and I gotta stay here and take care of you until I deem it a waste of resources. We don't have painkillers or antibiotics, but we have some understanding of our local botany. Certain leaves actually disinfect and speed up the healing process; quite amazing. It doesn't really feel all that real, but what does that matter anymore, right?" she said with a smirk.

"Is there any way you can untie me?" Carli finally uttered with shadowy innocence.

"It's not my call sweetie, sorry," she responded delicately.

"Can you at least loosen them?" Carli asked.

"That's not my call either," the plump woman snapped with a widening smile.

"So, what the fuck is your call?" Carli's rage began to surface, dissolving her thespian veil.

"Listen, honey . . . you can blame me for not letting you out or giving you a chance to escape being a woman and all, or you can understand that I am helping you. I'm doing everything I can without risking my life because, news flash sweetie, I care about my life a little more than I do about yours." Their eyes met like gunslingers ready to duel.

Eventually, Carli let out, ". . . Fair enough," as she rested her head back and loosened her grips on the armrests. There was a mutual respect now in the air, and the tension began to fade.

"I thought I was the last girl on Earth," Carli said in a genuine tone.

"It isn't really Earth anymore, but I thought the same thing, especially after all the girls these savages have been through," the plump woman replied, replacing her politeness with subtle cynicism. "So many girls, in the beginning . . . not all these men were animals before. Even the best, I hardly recognize now. You are the first woman we've found in over three years . . . the few we have left here are too broken. Some argued we needed to reproduce but, most I think never planned on raising any children." Carli began to grind her teeth in disgust. "I'm sorry; my name is Wendy, by the way."

"Carli . . . so, what's gonna happen with me?"

"Once I'm done takin' care of you, you'll join the comfort house. You seem tough though, like you'll last longer than the other poor souls," Wendy said, and she stared off, distracted. Suddenly, the door to the medical room was kicked in.

"Where's my woman?" the leader with the red beard yelled as he stomped in.

"Don't fucking kick it in like that! How many times Cliff, how many goddamn times do I have to tell you? I could be behind the fucking door!" Wendy started to yell and swing her arms dramatically.

"I'm sorry, Jesus fucking Christ!" Cliff yelled back, ending with a grizzly smile. He then strolled up and lifted her into the air effortlessly. She seemed small, momentarily, and her half-hidden smile lightly glinted.

"Okay babe, okay, put me down," she said calmly. He put her large body down and they kissed.

"She looks cleaned up," he said while Carli eyed him up and down with the fury of hell.

"Yeah, but she can't really move just yet," Wendy said quickly. Cliff kept quiet, locking his gaze on Carli for a moment, analytically.

". . . this takes too much time, or we use up too much shit, she's gonna have to deal with it," he said with cruel disregard.

"I know," she muttered. He then left just as loud as he came, slamming the door and stomping away.

"That's your man? So, you're the fucking queen then, huh?" Carli pointed out. Wendy remained silent. "I just need an opportunity and I can take care of everything else . . . please, give me a chance!"

"Lower your voice, child," Wendy said softly. Carli gloomed and her skin paled. "Why do you think I'm still here? Why do you think he's in charge?" Wendy looked at her icily. "The only reason he is in charge of these animals is because they want him to be . . . they love him, they respect him, and they fear him. If any of that changes even for a split second, everything we've built crumbles. I do not love this world and I do not love the man he has become, but pretending my old Cliff's still in there and holding it all together is the only way we'll get through this," she said.

"And then what?" Carli asked. Wendy looked at her, confused. "What happens after you get through this?" Carli persisted as Wendy's gaze dropped to the ground.

"I cannot change the world, sweetie, but I can get the next generation ready." Wendy rested her hand against her engorged belly. Carli looked at her and understood.

"I thought you were just a big lady," she stated sarcastically.

"I am, bitch, but not this big," Wendy sassed back with a subtle grin. Carli reciprocated the smile.

"When are you due?"

"Probably not for another month or two."

"Are you scared?" Carli asked. She once would have considered the prospect of children, but they were now just an afterthought; the world and her womb alike were too barren.

"I cannot wait," Wendy replied with an expanding smile. "I'm gonna let you rest and I'll be back in the morning. A gentleman named Randyll is going to watch you, but he'll stay outside the door. He's one of the few I like; you'll be safe." Wendy began to gather a few of her things together and headed for the door. Before she left, Carli thanked her genuinely. She smiled back, though Carli noted the effort it required.

Carli lay on the stretcher with eyes like saucers glued to the ceiling, all but forgetting the ceiling was there. She strayed into deep thought halfway through the night until she realized she was wasting precious time. She scanned the room and saw nothing practical that could be weaponized. She struggled desperately through her restraints and made some minor progress on her wrists. Then the door opened slowly, and a scrawny figure came in and closed the door behind him. He sat down in the dark and inspected Carli with a gaze she could feel.

"Can I fucking help you?" Carli asked in a Carli-like manner.

"Yeah you can actually," the voice bounced back with some irritation. "You're making noise, and noise attracts attention.

This job is my one and only chance to get some peace and quiet. Now, I'm going to have to ask you, please, stop trying to escape." She traced his silhouette with her eyes and remained quiet. "Obviously I understand why, but . . . there are at least thirty guys here who all cuddle up with their guns at night and would fuckin' love a chance to punish a comfort girl," the gentleman warned.

"What the fuck did you just call me?" Carli barked with disdain.

"I'm sure Wendy already told you." The man stood up to ignite a lantern in the corner of the room. "Might as well, I feel a conversation coming on." The light revealed a brittle man retreating back to his seat, ready to indulge in a late-night conversation with a prisoner. He had a weary yet peaceful face; bony and precise in all the right places. His skin spoke of youth, but his eyes of age. "I heard what they did to you and—"

"Where'd you get all the guns and ammo?" Carli interrupted. The skinny man looked at her, unsure where to start.

"Most of these men were in a special elite unit that prioritized getting high-value targets out of hot spots. Cliff was in command. When those visitors left us to fend for ourselves and people stepped out from the shadows again, our world was left crumbled. There was nothing to be seen but smoke and fire, and then storm. While remnants of the government were telling us to regroup and save political families, Cliff hatched another idea: Why don't we save our own? Most were gone without a trace. Others were found, but only a few were alive; mostly those who hid underground in shelters or tunneled freeways. My pops was one of Cliff's lieutenants, and he gave his life to get me here . . . made sure I was safe," the sorrowful skeleton explained.

"Jeez, all I asked was where you got the guns," Carli mumbled. The scrawny man could not help but chuckle.

"What about you? Let's talk about you."

Carli shook her head. "I'd rather just hear the rest of your boring story." She half-smiled at him, and her charm brightened the room. The man beamed and began again.

"We stayed on the road, always moving . . . we even had a helicopter early on, helped us find and build this place. The storms took it away from us, but not before we looted and scavenged everything within a one-hundred-mile radius of here, or at least it seemed," he continued.

"So, you guys are pretty well stocked on things other than guns, too?" Carli inquired, intrigued.

"You could say that," he slyly replied, but then his tone shifted at hearing the laughter and scuffles of jostling brutes outside, "but, things have been getting a little crazier here lately. Lot of infighting, people looting and abandoning . . . more and more executions. Someone even burned a field of ready crops, no one knows who or why . . . guess only time will tell what'll happen to this place. Wonder what my pops would think."

Carli began to look sick while her thoughts weighed heavy. "I wasn't going to ask, but if you heard, you might know. What happened to my friends?" she asked, dropping her sights to the floor.

"Same thing that's gonna happen to us all," Carli's new companion stated cynically. "My name's Randyll by the way, I usually start with that."

Carli looked at him with sunken brows. "Cool."

"Cool is a perfect name for you," Randyll said with a smile.

"Try smiling knowing you're going to be 'comforting' some sick fucks soon," Carli spat, coming to terms with the inevitability. The hair on Randyll's neck pricked like an angry cat's.

"You think you're the only one?" he asked, and she looked at him in surprise. "I'm probably not the only gay one here, but I'm definitely the only one man enough to admit it. Thing is, soon as I did, this fuckwad Donnie, who's still my roommate by the way, 'confided' in me, knowing I would understand; and when I respectfully refused his advances, he beat me and raped the shit out of me. Everyone gets raped—everyone—before they die. Even this world got raped before it died, and we were there to see every sickening moment . . . damn it." He began to grind his canines. "What would you do if you were out?" he thought aloud, then raised a brow to the pretty, sharp-tongued girl.

"Anything I can . . ." she said slyly.

"You know what . . . fuck this! You are quite convincing. Me and you, we're getting the fuck out of here, tomorrow night. Just have to get a few things in order . . ." he said, then swiftly exited the room. Carli remained silent, grinning with confusion at Randyll's sudden change of heart.

Chapter IV – Thoughts and Shadows

The following night Carli waited for Randyll to show. She was anxious—he'd given her no plan to think on, but she had a lot on her mind. She thought of Shane, and then what Bastian had said to her at Leonard's burial. Memory took her away, beyond the harsh years on the road and before the day she tried to forget, the day that changed everything. She recalled another time she had lacked a plan. When she had just finished high school and her boyfriend and all her friends were headed off to college, she was not. No one had ever pushed her to be better, to be strong, to work toward something, until he did. One day, smoking on her porch, she was approached.

"Hello. I'm your new neighbor. My name is Shane Fredericks." She looked up at him; he looked proud and strong, but sounded wise and delicate. "Are your parents home?" he asked.

"Nope," Carli snapped and continued to puff on her cigarette.

"Oh, well, you are all welcome to come by sometime for dinner. We are right next door if you need anything." His smile seemed bright and dreamy. Carli scoffed and looked away. As he walked away, she looked back at him. Something about him made her smile, and she tried to pin it on the funny way he moved. On that day, she never would have guessed what would become of them. He would tutor her, despite her flirtatious and rebellious nature, and help her land a job. He would even help her with her heroin problem.

"Drugs are for people who've already given up. Those too weak to face the realities of life. No one cares whether you'll make it or not; no one but me. But I can't help you, Carli. I will not help you. It's up to you if you want to die, alone and miserable, or if you think it's worth waking up and finding something to live for, something to be proud of, something to enjoy . . . someone to love." The anger and frustration had seeped into his tone. It was all he'd needed to say to her.

The memory began to dissipate like a broken cloud.

Back in the present, she thought her tears had run out, but she found another steady stream running from her eyes. Suddenly, the door creaked open and Randyll entered, pushing a cart in that rattled with glass vials and metalware. She quickly blinked her eyes in an attempt to dry them up.

"I brought some clothes for you," said Randyll as he lifted a folded outfit off the top of the cart.

"Wendy came by today and gave me some already," Carl said, sounding almost unappreciative.

"Oh, well, we'll take them anyway."

"What's up with the cart?" she asked, observing the flimsy thing. It had two tiers, a top shelf by the handlebar, and a bottom that was just above the wheels.

"What do you think?" Randyll asked with a grin. "You're gonna get under there while I drape this over you." He grabbed a folded tablecloth from the bottom and presented it. "Hopefully, we can just waltz right out of here."

Carli inspected the cart doubtfully but said nothing. Randyll cut through her leather restraints with a seatbelt cutter. She rung her wrists and ankles once free—the skin was itchy and sore—and then reluctantly climbed onto the bottom shelf of the cart. She had to curl herself into a ball and hold her legs in tightly to fit. It was uncomfortable, but better than the stretcher she was finally free from.

"Don't make a sound and be patient; we have to play along if I get snagged or questioned by someone," Randyll said. Carli kept still and quiet. Randyll lifted all the glass and metal and placed it back once the black tablecloth was on. He paused for a moment, making sure everything was in place. As he grabbed the handlebar, his hands shook uncontrollably. Randyll smiled nervously. "You got this . . . come on," he said to himself, but this did little to stop his tremors. He creaked the door open and pushed the cart through.

The hallway was dimly lit with candles and a bigger source of light coming from the vestibule up ahead. Randyll closed the door behind him and proceeded to lock it, growing more anxious with the clinks of the keys. He strode through, past doors and snoring men until he came upon the great light. It looked like a sun by the ceiling; a large chandelier with five branches and five burning lights. In the center was a living flame above a bulbous candle. The hallway opened up to a greeting room of some sort with couches and a bar, but all Randyll could see was the exit door. His eyes went straight over a man sitting and drinking alone.

"It's pretty late to do the lady's work," the man said with a hollow tune and raspy voice.

"Woah, hey . . . I forgot you were there." Randyll stiffened and his skin seemed to pale.

The man eyed him harder and sunk his brows. "You just walked by me a moment ago."

"Yeah, well . . . anyway, Wendy wanted me to check on the

girl and grab something."

"What'd she need?" he asked, strangely hungry for the answer.

"Don't think she'd appreciate me sharing that with you," said Randyll defiantly.

"Piss off then!" the man growled. As Randyll confidently rolled by, the man's eyes seemed to glint like brown embers. "Wait a second . . . that cloth, what are you hiding under there?"

Randyll turned and drew a pistol, small and concealable. "Come on then, let's go see Wendy . . . and you can fuckin' ask her." Randyll bared his fangs and loomed over the sitting drunk. The man's eyes squinted and looked away. He went back to drinking.

When they exited the room, they were under a white awning and the porch was bordered by a short cobblestone wall. A stairway of four steps led off into grass and dirt. The night air seemed thin. At the stairway, he lifted the front side, letting the back of the cart take the brunt of each step. The glass and metal rattled with every drop. Carli's hand shot out from the cloth to hold herself upright before she fell. As she did, she accidentally tugged on the tablecloth, and a glass vial fell and shattered against the stone railing. Silence followed and Randyll stood still, frozen, almost too scared to breathe. After some minutes passed, he fixed the tablecloth and went on, dragging the cart through flat dirt and patches of grass and weeds. Suddenly, a whistle bolted through the dark and Randyll froze again.

"I was wondering where you were off to, hmm." The man hummed at the end of each sentence, melodically, but as if a hidden pain forced it out. He was a large brute with puckered lips and eyes that reflected the moonlight.

"What do you want, Donnie?" Randyll asked with fettered annoyance and a lingering fear.

"For you to stop playing hard to get, hmm."

"I'll be home soon." Randyll tried to assure him.

"Where are you heading, hmm?" asked Donnie.

Randyll stayed quiet for a moment and swallowed his disgust. "Come on, let's make this quick," he said reluctantly. Donnie smiled, and a starved malice boiled behind the expression. Randyll led him past the buildings, to a spot darker than most by the back perimeter gate. There was a grassy slope before the gate that led to a bed of daisies—among other unknowable flowers—and mushrooms. Donnie sniffed the back of Randyll's neck, and Randyll felt the tip of his nose brush against his pricked-up hairs.

"Leave the cart aside, hmm," Donnie said, sounding over-zealous.

Randyll turned to face him, looking grave and sad. "I'm sorry, Donnie." Donnie looked confused, even when he saw the gun in Randyll's hand, aimed at him. When Randyll shot him, his confused look remained unchanged. He dropped and groaned and eventually released his final hum.

"Great plan!" Carli shouted and crawled out from the cart. They could already hear the men shouting, and then a siren went off, crying over the forest. Carli started to climb the gate, but Randyll grabbed her arm and pulled her away. A few feet up ahead was an opening Randyll had made just for them the previous night. The siren rang out and men searched, but they found only a dead Donnie and a cart.

Chapter V – No Man's Land

Bastian woke to find Shane the restless already awake, staring at the remains of a fire. "How's the arm?" Bastian yawned.

"You mean what used to be an arm?" Shane said calmly without lifting his gaze from the burnt logs. "The pain takes its toll, but it's not unbearable."

"Good. We shouldn't be far," Bastian said confidently as he started to pack up his withered gear.

"Bastian, I've been thinking . . . they cannot find us before we find them. We can't underestimate these people. They're well armed, we know that already . . . for all we know, they could be watching us right now." Bastian stopped and turned to face him.

"What are you suggesting?" he inquired coldly.

"We stop following these tracks and try to find a slightly less conventional path in the same direction. We head a few miles south before we start heading west again."

"What if we take too long, Shane?" Bastian asked, annoyed. "What if she's dead by the time we get there?"

Shane whipped his focus toward the hulking man to look him dead in the eye and said, "They don't want her dead . . . remember?"

Bastian stood sternly and took a few intimidating steps

toward his old friend, but neither backed down. "If Carli hasn't opened her stupid mouth and gotten herself killed yet, it's only a matter of time," he explained until a series of coughs and wheezes ransacked his lungs.

"We're both cripples now. So, let's be smart about this," Shane said with an apologetic shift in his presence as he watched the great man recoil and gasp and seemingly shrink in size. Bastian, still trying to gather his words and breath, could only nod in agreement. They altered their path, but not their destination.

They trudged throughout the entirety of the day, until the sun fell and the sky dusked. As twilight lingered, they found a shallow bluff shelter that curved out over a patch of grass. A bundle of bamboo-like plants sprouted from atop the bluff. Inside was a small mound of dirt and a depression behind it. "Let's camp here. We need rest and shouldn't be limping throughout the night," Shane said. Bastian just collapsed and remained on the ground, defeated.

"I'll keep first watch. Can't move but can't sleep either," the gentle giant huffed.

"I'll get some wood. We can probably keep the flame hidden in here." Shane rested his gear and mobilized to search the general vicinity. The forest seemed hollow and quiet, and yet, watchful. It didn't take long to gather what they needed for a fire despite the dying light. Shane emerged from the shadows and was immediately welcomed by a paranoid Bastian with a knife cocked in his hand. Shane dropped his catch of branches and twigs and put his hand forward.

"What the fuck?" he whispered.

Bastian lowered the blade in relief. ". . . We are being watched," he said as Shane gave him a studying look.

The violet moon left the land alone in its darkness and the

two remained silent, perpetually lost in delirium, fevers, and a sleepless night. The cold without the radiation of a fire began to chip away at them. An alien howl echoed in the distance. Suddenly, a conifer cone hit Bastian directly on his forehead.

"Aw! Fuck you, coward!" he blasted as he swung his fists blindly against shadows until he tripped on one of the branches Shane had left lying in the dirt.

"Shhh!" Shane insisted. The vast canopy began to rustle.

"Are they in the trees?" Bastian whispered. They both glanced upward and realized their vision wasn't going to help them for the time being.

"If it was them, they wouldn't be so hesitant on attacking us by now; they outnumber and outgun us, so . . . why would they play with us?" Shane started to rationalize.

"It's the dark, wouldn't be smart to do anything at all right now . . . maybe they think we have more," Bastian rebutted.

"I don't know. I'm starting to think it might not be human," Shane said, staring off.

"I don't even know what's worse anymore," Bastian muttered under his skipping breath.

A wet sound, sudden and conspicuous, lathered behind their chatter. The two survivors slowly turned to face their rustling gear. Shane found a fallen cone in the shade like a blind man with a stick and chucked it toward the noise. A distressed squeal like a harpooned dolphin sang out as it ran off. Almost immediately, the squeal began to multiply and echo into a thousand voices barraging the woods with powerful waves.

"Fucking run!" Shane yelled as he dashed through the bushes, crashing sightlessly through the commotion. Bastian followed and dove into Shane's back blindly. They both tumbled for a few feet, getting hooked and snagged by the bony arms and hands of a splintering thicket. In the black, they found their feet again.

"Our shit!" Bastian exclaimed. Small objects whistled through the wind, cracked trees, and left the rich flora in tatters. Rocks, pinecones, monstrous seeds bigger than a fist, and whatever else was soon turned into ammunition against them.

"We'll come back, but there's nothing we can do now," Shane barked, winded. The squeals and howls bounced off each other, forming a frenzied choir while the canopy swayed. The two found cover in a ditch half-tucked underneath a waning oak with draping vines and listened to the screams in the distance.

"We gotta . . . go back," Bastian said between desperate clutches at air.

"I know," Shane replied reluctantly.

The two suffered another seemingly endless night without sleep or peace. The crack of dawn gave rise to an eerie fog that embraced the forest. As they crawled out of hiding, a ferocious roar erupted from within Bastian, like a bear clawing out of his stomach. Shane lifted his brows, thinking of all the times he had failed the group; thinking of his incompetence as a leader.

"I'm starving, we need to find water, my head feels like it's caving in, and my vision is starting to blur," Bastian greeted the morning with resentment, roughly massaging his bristled scalp.

"Fog's not gonna help. Which direction did we run in?" Shane responded while his eyes scanned their surroundings. Eventually they spotted the bush they'd crashed through and headed in that direction. The ground was hardly visible through the morning murk, thick as snow. Shane suddenly stepped on something soft and juicy. He kneeled to get a closer look, and then a clearing in the fog revealed a dead tree squid drenched in a navy blue puddle of blood. The creature's soft skin was a dark shade of lavender, decorated all around with black freckles and maroon moss.

"Jesus Christ," Bastian said as he found five similarly tangled corpses outside the bluff shelter. "They must've gotten trampled or something while they were fighting over our stuff." Bastian saw an empty backpack and looked through it fruitlessly. "Do they have can openers or something, for fuck's sake! How would they know to take those?" Bastian asked as Shane picked up another empty pack that was barely hanging together by threads. He threw it off in the distance indignantly.

"I guess they can open canteens too," Shane relayed.

"Luckily not . . . check this out," Bastian said as he held up one of their canteens, half full. He picked up a crushed can of tuna, dripping and frothing. Shane's relief lifted him back into the motion of fighting gravity. Bastian opened the canteen for Shane in consideration of his new handicap, knowing he would be too proud to ask. They each took a moment to rehydrate, but the source was too scarce. After slapping the canteen repeatedly to empty every last drop, the two survivors shamefully took turns lapping up salty tuna water from the punctured can they found amongst the raid. "Should we try one of these things?" Bastian put forth the idea disquietly.

"Fuck it, all the wood I gathered is probably still here," Shane said as he went around sorting through the scattered supplies amidst the grounded clouds. Bastian picked up a lifeless cephalopod and skewered it on a makeshift spit.

The fire bloomed eventually and burned gracefully. The meat began to singe and then crackle and pop over flickering orange lashes and plumes. They watched their tantalizing meal to come, salivating for salvation, and were finally rewarded with the fruits of their labor.

"How is it?" Shane asked with a mouthful, although he already knew the answer.

Bastian cleared his throat, ripped off another piece covered in tiny suckers, and began to masticate the rubbery substance. ". . . Tastes like shit," he said plainly.

"Seriously," Shane agreed while they both continued to feast, despite it being so bitter and unpalatable. Afterward, the two gathered up their remaining supplies into the one pack left intact and continued on their quest. The fog continued to weigh them down.

A few miles down, Bastian collapsed to his knees and trembled. "Come on, we gotta keep moving while there's still daylight," Shane lamented, concerned. Bastian did not, however, respond. ". . . Bastian?"

Shane approached his colleague until the giant put up his hand, bringing him to a halt and keeping him at bay. Immediately after, he spewed a blue acidic fluid along with morsels of string and rubber. He continued violently and vehemently. "Holy shit! Are you okay?" Before Shane could get a response, a succession of rapid gunfire belched in the wind. Shane spun frantically, trying to pinpoint the direction of the shots while Bastian continued to retch and puke. The blasting became more apparent and obnoxious. "Stay here!" Shane commanded as he stalked like a jungle cat through the fog toward the chaos.

Bastian attempted to interject, but his sickness interrupted and overwhelmed him. Shane could hear a few crazed men yelling indistinctly in the distance. Suddenly, the canopy began to shudder in a familiar manner.

With every crouched step, Shane heard the gunshots nearing,

followed by the dissonance of deathly howls.

"Come on you lil' sea monkeys, you wanna test whose fucking wild this is?" a stranger bellowed no more than twenty feet from Shane, but the fog was on no one's side. Various objects were pelted at the man from above, and the woods began to crack and cry. He responded by firing heedlessly at the treetops. Shane kept low, hunting the voice, and a squid fell inches away, pulped and soggy, writhing its arms in a desolate attempt to grab its fleeting life force. Shane had his hunting knife in his right hand—his only hand. The murk pushed past a silhouette and Shane could see his target. He crept up to the shouting man and silenced him with precision. Shane unsheathed the blade from the man's neck and let him drop to the floor to bleed out. The fallen gun splashed in his blood and was painted red on one side.

Shane cleaned the slick blade against the man's shirt and searched through the corpse's pockets. He found three cigarettes in a pack along with a gold-plated Zippo lighter, a half-eaten granola bar that he immediately took a bite from as he continued looking, and a broken pocket watch that he left on the floor. He then continued to take off the dead man's boots to replace his own tattered shoes. Shane then loaded the last clip in the gun, maddened that the spiteful man had wasted so much.

The screeching persisted, accompanied by the sound of a shotgun blasting through the upper level of the land. Shane then noticed steps built into one of the titan trees. He used the rifle's strap to hang the gun over his good shoulder while he pushed himself through an incredible struggle of climbing the steps with limited grab space one-handed. He pressed his cauterized nub into holds with his weight, and it started to bleed. In the trek up the giant tree, which was seemingly endless, Shane began to lose hope that he would ever make it to the top. His thoughts were interrupted with a boot to the head that almost knocked him off, but he resisted the force.

"Oh shit, Jack? That you?" Shane ignored the question in the air, grateful for the fog hiding him from the mysterious voice. "Jack! Don't fucking shoot blindly up here you fucking dumb prick, you're gonna kill us." Shane suddenly grabbed the man's ankle and pulled him off the tree with all his might. His wails were piercing and unknowing. The mist pretended to catch him multiple times until he met the punishing ground. Shane lost his own balance and dropped the gun, but caught himself a few pegs down. He realized that he had to go back; his handicap would most likely get him killed if he continued up. When his struggle was finally over and he eventually got to the base of the tree, he found a curious Bastian with a cyan-speckled smile.

"You didn't make it to the top, did you?" Bastian asked sarcastically, his voice raspy.

"I thought I could; took this guy down instead for some questioning," Shane said, glistening with blood, sweat, and failure.

"I don't think there's going to be any questioning from him," Bastian said, pointing to a pile of twisted limbs, bones, and guts. "You were high enough to do some damage though . . . nice," Bastian added. "Clean the nub, I'll find out what's up there." Bastian looked up into nothingness and then hocked a blue viscous spitwad.

Shane sat against the tree, feeling useless. Around forty-five minutes into Bastian's ascent up the wooden column, Shane's silence was broken by two bodies falling from the heavens with hideous impacts. The dead lay quiet, not a few feet from him, neither of them Bastian. The fog began to fade, and so did his concern, but the world above was still shrouded. Shane began to doze off, sleep-deprived, and hazily woke to the breeze carrying the voice of a man, raucous and thundering, and then nothing. A sustained moment of silence rolled through the tension. Suddenly, the woods began to break and fall from the sky, chopped away by the relentless stuttering of a heavy machine gun.

After disposing of two guards, Bastian had further trouble breathing, and his sprained ribs began to restrict him like a python. Still, he made it to the top. He rested in an elaborate tree fort littered with supplies, including ammunition, knives, water, radio transceivers, grenades, and a set of keys that Bastian sorted through. He then gathered his strength and pressed on.

The labyrinth had rope bridges connecting a network of trees, each with platforms and railings; it was one outpost that stretched its reach out far, looking down at the world. A familiar presence stroked Bastian's peripheral vision. He looked toward a bridge and saw a man sitting in the center with his legs hanging off to one side, downing a dusty bottle of cheap Vodka. The man then proceeded to throw the bottle in the distance once it was dry. It was the grim man who had so kindly offered Bastian mercy. The bridge began to sway and tremble, but he was too deep in thought and too intoxicated to really think on it, with no reason to believe it was anyone other than one of his fellow comrades. Bastian continued to creep toward him, noticing he wasn't responding to the bridge's seismic activity. By the time the grim man realized what was happening, Bastian had his blade to his throat.

"What the fuck?" he said, disoriented.

"Where is she?" Bastian demanded.

"Who?" the man persisted.

"The girl you watched get raped!"

The grim man's gaze wandered aimlessly. ". . . She's gone," he whispered.

"The fuck you mean?" Bastian's wrath began to radiate like a fiery aura.

"She escaped . . . been gone for . . . a day, maybe more. One of ours helped her. They'll find her though, unless she passes our borders, if so . . . then she's someone else's problem."

Bastian took a minute to process this new information while he continued his constant struggle to respire. ". . . Let me put you to rest, brother," he then recited. The grim man took a moment, acknowledging his remembrance.

"You can have all the time you want brother, but it'll never be enough. I'm ready for some peace." He lifted his chin, ready for his execution. Bastian hesitated, pondering his words, but eventually dragged the knife across the man's skin, releasing his blood and misery. Bastian then nudged him off the bridge, and the body dove down headfirst.

Bastian crossed the bridge, now completely lost, looking for his way back.

"You think I can't see you!" a sadistic voice rang out, and Bastian froze. Suddenly, the sound of a heavy machine gun rolled through the air.

Bastian dropped to the floor and waited for the fire to cease, but it was persistent. Accompanied by the metallic blare was a man howling like a wolf and laughing through the smoke. The berserk screeches of the tree squid troop answered back. Bastian noticed the bullets weren't flying in his direction, and he started crawling toward the triggerman.

The gunfire and the laughing grew louder as Bastian crawled across yet another bridge. He arrived at a vibrating platform, held together by planks and two by fours. The sadistic cackling came from a man stationed inside a fortified weapon mount that was unleashing endlessly and aimlessly into the vast canopy. Cephalopods, branches, and the rest of the riled ecosystem high up in the forest crowns were evicted, thrown to the ground or disintegrated from this plane of existence.

Bastian pulled the pin from a grenade he'd taken and rolled it gently at the gun turret; he then immediately stood up and ran across the bridge. The shooter felt Bastian's presence and movements. He stopped firing and turned around, only for a white flash to bleach his vision and devour him in flame. Bastian did not have enough time to fully cross the bridge. The explosion destroyed the foundations of one side, and the bridge fell limp, and Bastian with it. He managed to grab hold before it slammed him into a tree. The pain in his bones became apparent again, and his grip weakened. He started to slide down, burning his palms against the rope. He stopped himself for a moment, but found he could not hold on any longer. He let go and landed ten feet down, though he could not recall the impact. His vision blurred and his ears ceased to work. His eyes shut for a supposed second and opened again to see Shane grabbing at his collar, yanking him upward with his only hand. He seemed distraught, mouthing worry and wonder, though Bastian could not hear what he was saying. "She escaped . . ." Bastian murmured, ". . . she made it." The broken giant then continued to pass out.

Moments later, a deafening wail pulled him back to the waking world; sirens were crying out over the forest, and Shane was dragging him along, with great effort and desperation.

Chapter VI – The King of Hell

"How much farther until you chill the fuck out?" Carli inquired between gasps of breath.

"We have to be completely out of the zone before they find us . . . we both know what happens if they do," Randyll insisted.

"The zone?"

"The zone is our territory. We encountered another group on the road. Things got bad . . . almost escalated into a full-blown war. We outgunned them, but they outnumbered us. Finally, Cliff and the other leader set up an agreement; nobody was to cross into the other's lands, and that was that," Randyll explained.

"So, we are going into their territory so your people will stop following us? That sounds sketchy as shit," Carli growled.

"We just need to lose them at the border, then we split and don't stop until there aren't any people anywhere," Randyll said, looking into the distance while Carli remained unpleased. The two wandered through the woods, presumably following a map they had stolen before their escape. Randyll constantly looked up and down to verify consistency between the symbols and the surrounding environment. "Hold up, I'm confused," he said, lost in the map's lines and shapes.

Carli rolled her eyes and plopped down on a large boulder

spotted with blood algae and lined with patterned fissures. He began to pace back and forth, muttering to himself. Carli noticed a prominent green rose sprouting out of a crack in the boulder. It had an outer layer of petals that draped low, covering the stem like the dress of a seductress. She plucked it from the stone and blew it with the passing zephyr as it breezed by. It spun and cut through the air while the flower's dress turned into a parachute, swaying back and forth like Newton's cradle before it gently landed.

Suddenly, the boulder began to shake, and Carli hopped off instinctively. "Jesus fuck! What the hell?" she yelled. The two froze, their attention captured by the trembling rock. A pair of alien compound eyes lifted their lids and began to rise from the crag. A silver lobster tail unraveled from underneath, and a left-handed claw cracked out from the side, elephantine and dwarfing its miniscule twin on the right. Eight spider legs lifted the creature up, and it began to slowly crawl away while Carli and Randyll watched in disbelief, like deer caught in the bright.

The sunlight began to wash away but lingered like an ember's glow. "We're lost, huh?" Carli asked rhetorically.

". . . Yeah, we were always lost," Randyll said grudgingly. "Do you have any more water? I'm all out." Carli tossed him a nearly empty canteen.

"Let's set up camp," she said, taking charge, which Randyll was happy to comply with. A flame was given life and a pot of water reached its boiling point. They took the water off the heat and waited for it to cool. The effort proved difficult; they were much too dehydrated and impatient to wait a reasonable amount of time, so they drank the near-scalding hot water. "We need to hunt or scavenge in the morning. I think we've put enough miles between us and those motherfuckers," Carli hissed with a burnt tongue, exhausted.

"I hope so. I'll keep first watch," Randyll said, much to her relief.

Still beautiful, Carli looked harder, paler, and years older every passing moment. She loved to sleep; it was the one thing she looked forward to, day after day. She was always too beat and sleepless to be compromised by any dreams or nightmares—just blankness, silence, and peace.

"Sounds good to me," she said tiredly, then proceeded to lay in the cold dirt and put a backpack under her head as a pillow. Carli fell asleep to the soft whisper of steam and vapor as Randyll killed the flame; the suppression of fire briefly masking the anxious noise in the backdrop.

"Wake up beautiful, and my, aren't you beautiful? I think I've seen you in a dream before." A smooth yet eerily familiar voice crept in with the morning before Carli could open her crusted eyes. As she did, her blurry vision began to focus. She was surrounded by boots and bitter men armed to the teeth, survivalists with crowbars, axes, and baseball bats. One man even carried a steel sword, and another a chainsaw. Carli's eyes began to overflow.

"Shhh . . . don't cry, I got you," the voice lured her attention back and a cold, gritty hand wiped a tear off her cheek. He was a relatively young man, with beige skin and webbed scars over his exposed hands and neck. A loose white shirt draped over his black long-sleeved under armor, and the streaks and stains of dried blood swirled like the face of a peppermint. His steel-tipped work boots dug at the ground and flickered with silver-bladed tongues sewn in at the edges of the toes. The protruding blades were also spattered with red droplets. Sheathed in his belt were two colossal knives, one a heavy cleaver with a slight chip and the other a thin serrated chef's blade; they were the most prominent of his decorations, his silent sisters, or so they were known amongst the men. Lastly, strapped to his back and shoulder was a black leather holster that carried a Beretta M9.

Randyll was on his knees with a man behind him holding the chainsaw steady. "Are you a part of Cliff's crew?" the young leader asked, but Randyll immediately interjected.

"Slugger please, we met on the road, I left those guys."

The leader turned to him with an angry smile. "Am I fucking talking to you right now?" He started to approach Randyll. "I can see everything I want to know in your pathetic little eyes, so shut the fuck up!" Randyll looked down with such trepidation he seemed to be corroding.

". . . Slugger?" Carli asked.

The leader turned to face her with an ever-widening grin and a darkness deep in his bright green eyes. "I wouldn't have chosen it myself, but a title is something you earn, right?" he sneered.

"Is it really you?" Carli asked. He scoffed. "It's me, Carli . . ." She stopped herself, unsure of how else to put it. His smile faded, and for a split second she could almost sense the murderous rage within him, though he immediately put the flames out and forced a grin back up.

"Well then, why don't you come back with us?" Slugger inquired.

"Can my friend come?" she asked, hopeful.

"Him?" He pointed to Randyll. "I wish I could tell that face yes, but I cannot." Carli looked at him, confused. Slugger walked over to Randyll, not stopping until they were face to face. "Whether or not he is here to spy, kill me, steal from us, or fuck, I don't know . . . give us valuable information even, I can't have that. Cliff and I prevented a fucking war! That doesn't mean shit if we can just waltz up into each other's territory. Fuck yeah we are savages, but that doesn't mean we still can't be civil. Never have we—not once!—crossed those fucking lines. It's an arrangement that should be taken seriously. Everything over here is ours, but we aren't selfish, are we boys?" he finished with a fiendish taunt while his men began to laugh under their breaths. "I think we'll just take a hand." Drool seeped past the corners of his snarled lips. Carli stood up and attempted to approach the maniac, his familiarity starting to fade. Before she had a chance, the majority of his men stepped in front of her. "Whoa, whoa guys, easy. What's up, beautiful?" he asked with a tilted head and a squinted look.

"First off, my name is not fucking beautiful, it's Carli. Second, your name is not Slugger, and third, Randyll hates Cliff more than any of you, except me," Carli said harshly and confidently. Slugger studied her, intrigued.

"Hmm . . . well alright Carli, I can respect that. Even though that might not be my name, you call me anything else and you'll fucking regret it." They looked into each other's eyes contemptuously, yet with a curiosity that could be mistaken for admiration. "And by the way, I don't hate Cliff. I respect the guy. It has nothing to do with that, anyway. Now can I please just take the guy's fucking hand already?"

Carli's stomach churned and her insides felt spoiled; her hatred for the world and its inhabitants peaked, and she no longer cared if the face before her was the one she remembered and once longed for. Slugger responded to her hellish fury with his trademark sadist simper, his faintly yellow teeth shining in the morning's glow.

"It's okay," Randyll said to Carli, defeated.

"See, it's okay." Slugger began to pace. "Now what the hell can I use to chop a hand off?" He walked up to one of his soldiers flipping a hatchet around playfully. "Nah, that's too boring." He continued his stroll through his group and came upon a man with a machete. "Where's the challenge in that?" The soldier sniggered wickedly. He then came up to the man holding the chainsaw, the chromium teeth at Randyll's throat. "I feel déjà vu . . . wait a minute . . . this is perfect!" The man also carried a twelve-inch rusted hammer in his belt. Slugger took the liberty of taking the hammer out and ceremoniously held it up for everyone to see. His men guffawed like schoolyard bullies. "Looks like we got a winner. Set him up, please." The chainsaw man, along with another, grabbed hold of Randyll while a third brought out a chopping block. It was made out of an old tree stump with scarlet cuts and hacks of the past branded into the wood as if from a paintbrush. He grabbed Randyll's arm and forced it down.

"Please!" Carli pleaded desperately. Slugger pulled out his Beretta and pointed it at her.

"It's happening, Carli. So sit the fuck down before I change my mind about you."

"Fuck you!" Carli screamed. "Those fucking pieces of shit raped me! And fucking laughed about it!" Slugger lost his smile and stared at Carli, waiting for her to finish. "They locked me up as a sex slave and Randyll had balls big enough to help me escape." She stopped herself to catch her breath and wipe the salty streams from her face.

"You finished?" he asked, seemingly unfazed while she looked at him, broken and insignificant. "Okay than . . . motion denied!" His cruel smile crept back into place. He walked up to Randyll and whispered something in his ear. Randyll exhaled deeply and nodded in acceptance. Carli witnessed the exchange and found no use for further words. No one held Randyll down anymore; he voluntarily kept his arm in a convenient position. "Rules make us men . . . without them we are animals, fucking out in the open, killing and stealing from our own. This is necessary . . . we are necessary," the war chief recited the words, laws laid down even before his reign.

Slugger lifted the hammer in the light and brought it down, giving Randyll no time to react. The hammer struck his wrist and sunk in. It immediately started to blush and swell at an alarming rate. Randyll suffered through it all and managed to stick in his position. Slugger repeatedly hammered his wrist into the block of wood, taking blood and skin and bone fragments whenever he lifted the tool. The assailant was truly enjoying himself. Eventually, after more than several hacks, Randyll's hand was barely hanging together by strings of flesh and veins. His body struggled and his eyes started rolling up into his head. Slugger grabbed hold of his hand and yanked it off, then proceeded to throw it in the distance. He inhaled deeply, sniffing and tasting the atmosphere. He held an unsatisfied smirk as he sensually rubbed his erect phallus over his pants and looked off into the vast openness. He then turned around, stormed up to Randyll, and submerged the tool into his skull.

At first, it was hard for Carli to watch, but she found herself numb and empty by the end. She held her tongue and eased her scowl. Randyll's corpse fell lightly. The sadist ripped the hammer out and tossed the tool over to the chainsaw-wielding guard, who caught it along with a splash of blood.

"Thank you, Jim. Alright, now some of you faggots help me get him to the road."

"You gonna eat him?" Carli asked in teary disapproval.

"Not me," he said, scratching at the patchy stubble on his face, burned and ridden with sweat and soot.

Carli was unbound, and the crew didn't look at her or treat her as a prisoner. The host moved silent and careful through the forest. She remained off to the side, away from them but keeping them in sight. Carli began talking to herself, something she hadn't done in some time now. "What are you going to do? You gonna keep crying and pleading?" she muttered to herself. "What? . . . You're so weak. You actually thought about it, didn't you? You thought it might make it all easier. Kill yourself and it'll all be done with. What would he say to you right now?" As she asked herself the final question, she remembered Shane's words again. Another tear fell, but that only made her more frustrated. "It's still worth it," this time, Carli said to him. She suddenly remembered where she was and looked to her left to find a man curiously listening to her. He wasn't close enough to make out exactly what she had said, but he displayed great interest, nonetheless. She then decided to stay close to the man who led them.

"Where are we going?" she asked Slugger resentfully. He ignored her curiosity and her tone. "You gonna come after me if I run?" she then inquired.

Slugger lifted a brow, amused. "I thought you wanted to come with us?"

"It's not like I got a lot of choices," she scoffed back sharply.

"You got the whole fucking world to run around in . . . you've got all the choices," he said as he turned to face her, a goading yet friendly grin plastered on his face. She looked away, masking her doubt with a stone-cold face and leaving any traces of uncertainty in the dark matter of her mind.

They came to a crack in the woods, a lonely old-world road poking its head out from the dunes and weeds of time, and heard the hoarse chatter of men. "Where's my girl?" Slugger bellowed as he emerged from the trees. Standing tall and broad amongst a host of scattered vehicles, all empty and awaiting the return of their riders, was an impressive vessel: a silver truck crude with mud and faded paint. It carried another squadron in the flatbed. Outfitted with kill toys and firepower, they were there to guard the road and the abandoned vehicles for the returning party. The men grew deafly quiet, in awe of the angel before them. Carli shone a tempting light, and they ogled her like moths born in darkness; many of them had not seen a woman in years. Despite this, they knew their leader, and they knew better. She was his, off limits . . . forbidden fruit. With the exception of a few lingering eyes, most looked away with much effort.

Suddenly, Carli found herself frozen and speechless, as if she'd stepped into tar and forgotten how to speak. Up ahead, resting in shadow, a 1970 Chevrolet Corvette Stingray convertible, beaten and aged, gracefully smiled with the style of its era. Steering reins of rope, leather, and chain were fastened to the front. The reins were attached to two shelled reptilian monstrosities, similar to the wingless dragon that took Shane's limb. Their tails were forcefully coiled and hung behind them like scaled whips, tightly wound. The one on the left was muzzled with a crude restraint galvanized with black iron, while his mate on the right had her jaws free. The scouting group returned to their vehicles while Slugger approached his pets; Carli followed, keeping her distance. The muzzled beast snarled at Slugger through the breathing slits of his ferric mask.

"Fuck you too, Homer," he said, giving him a scowl. The

creature on the right, however, looked surprisingly pleased to see Slugger. "Hey, how's my lady," the warlord said in an uncharacteristically soft voice. He proceeded to rub the top of her head and scratch her chin. The dragon closed its eyes, poised and content. Carli observed in disbelief. Engines began to roar and men began to grunt. "Alright, alright you pricks," Slugger whispered to himself, annoyed. He hopped in the convertible and held his hand out for Carli to take.

"Seriously?" she asked, then shook her head in refusal.

"Fine, then you can walk or catch a ride with one of those smelly fucks." Slugger shrugged, unconcerned. She rolled her eyes and got in the car, slamming the door as she sat in the passenger's seat. Slugger smiled and tugged at the reins, commanding the beasts of burden to begin their haul. Half the large group split into the woodlands again and disappeared on foot.

The convoy was on the road almost an hour before Carli finally said something. "You're a sick piece of shit, you know that?"

Slugger chuckled in response. "Oh, don't I know it. Is that supposed to hurt my feelings or make me reevaluate my way of thinking?" He lifted his brow and smiled, seemingly aroused at the accusation.

"It's supposed to," she reiterated.

"I do enjoy the violence sometimes . . . it's in our nature, but what I do not enjoy is the chaos. A world like this . . . people really forget how important the principles are," he plainly stated.

"Bullshit," Carli insisted.

Slugger looked down the winding road and pictured a serpent; a great basilisk under his control. "Who knows, maybe

I am just delusional . . . but you know what the funny thing is? It doesn't even fucking matter." He held a seemingly happy smile, and Carli was unsure whether he was belittling her or himself, laughing at life, or asking for help.

"What happened to you?" she asked, somewhat concerned but more so simply curious. The madman remained silent, and Carli watched as the smile receded and a frustrated blankness in his face surfaced; and then the conversation was over. They eventually pulled into a camp spot already set up with three men feeding a gluttonous blaze.

A purple sliver of a moon welcomed the night and lent the land a dreamy magenta shade. Fifteen men sat around the fire, including Slugger with Carli by his side. The two dragons were off tethered to the great wooden pillars of the forest. The creatures were sharing a meal; pale and bone-stretched flesh had been ripped apart and was soaking the dirt. It was Randyll—dead, pulped, handless, and naked; he had been stripped of all his clothing so the beasts could digest him smoothly. Homer's muzzle had been removed. Before they freed his fangs, the men had fastened an intricate collar with spikes on the interior, prohibiting the creature from tugging on the leash. Carli watched them feast, contemplating her own numbness. She could not help but to feel somehow guilty over Randyll's fate, and the guilt only worsened as she tried to forget it.

"Hungry?" Slugger offered her a plate of mystery meat that she began to devour immediately, unconcerned. "Course you are . . . everyone is nowadays," he said before he started to destroy his own portion. Jim, the chainsaw wielder, broke through the crossing chatter and eventually garnered their total attention for his story.

"So it was me, Luke, and Big fuckin' Ben a few months back on a tracking mission. We were hunting something that was breaking into one of our slaughterhouses . . . slaughterhouse five, I think. The one by the mountain. We knew it was an animal by the way it busted in, sloppy as fuck. The trail led us to a goddamned cave. Me and Luke started talkin' 'bout how we gonna get it. Should we drop a boulder on its head, smoke it out, tripwire . . . you know, intricate stuff." His crowd chortled eagerly. Carli listened and Slugger admired her while she was distracted. She was familiar to him, and he could no longer deny it. She glowed, and he basked in it.

"Big freaky ass Ben . . . you know, the wordsmith that he is . . . just stood there ugly and scary as ever, not even acknowledging us, by the way—he randomly walks right into the cave in the middle of us planning it out, dead at night, in the snow, with no torch." The crowd grew quiet; even Slugger leaned forward. "It felt like a fuckin' hour passed by until we heard something, and suddenly . . ." After another suspenseful pause, Jim started to squeal and moan wildly, attempting to mimic a gorilla having intercourse. He then got up and started to motion his pelvis back and forth, pretending he was penetrating a bent over ape. Slugger spit out some food, unable to hold in his laughter, as the raucous crowd erupted. Carli looked around hesitantly with a smirk and giggle on her lips, and Jim continued.

"Then, there was some major spanking . . . and after that, sure enough, we heard some gargling." His audience wrinkled their faces in playful disgust, truly enjoying the entertainment, the distraction. "I swear, I am not making this shit up, you could have asked Luke before he got choked out over a pig, anyway . . . Eventually, after their passionate lovemaking was over, we heard some steps, and something being dragged . . . it was coming back toward us. Me and Luke were shittin' bricks not knowing what to do, but we stood our ground like real men . . . and what do you know, mother fucking creepy ass Ben pops out of the cave with a lifeless, hairy ass Cyclops-ape-thing the size of him . . . and we all know that's saying something. But hey, I guess you're just gonna have to take my word for it, because I wouldn't ask old Benny boy back home if he fucked a one-eyed yeti and snowcapped the snow man, if you know what I mean."

The men boomed and reclaimed the airwaves with their recreation, and Carli shook her head, trying to conceal her amusement. "Hey lady," an intoxicated older gentleman tried to get her attention. She glanced at him with mistrust. He held up a bottle of wine that he had been sipping on, offering it to her in a drunkard fashion. "Only the classy stuff for—" He belched a pungent odor before he could finish his thought.

Carli covered her nose, waved the air aside, and received his offer. "Cheers, old man," she said before chugging the bottle down to the last drop. "Alright, now that the pussy shit is gone, where's the good stuff?" Carli asked the guys before tossing the bottle into the black. It became apparent the crew was growing accustomed to her charm.

A few hours passed of drinking and stories, and Carli became visibly intoxicated. Slugger leaned toward her and revealed something he took out of his pocket. "Look what I got," he said trying to spark her interest. It was a glass pipe, clouded with colored swirls and stained with resin along with a small nugget of stale, dry marijuana. Carli was intrigued for a second until she saw a micro spider crawl out. It was pearl white and gone in a flash, burying back into the plant matter from whence it came.

"I'm gonna pass," she said, both disgusted and disappointed.

"Suit yourself." Slugger packed the nug tight and began to drag the fumes obliviously. He held the smoke in for a moment and then began to cough, gag, and spit. Carli could not contain her uproar. Slugger continued to retch and struggle but cracked a smile when he heard her laugh. She offered a waterskin that reeked with the stifling scent of homemade moonshine. It was a drink she was just introduced to and had quickly become fond of, but he shook his head in rejection.

"I don't think you've had a single drink in you this whole time," she pointed out.

"I don't drink, can't afford to," he said quickly, still recovering between coughs.

"Aren't you like, the king of hell around here?" she asked with a crooked coquettishness. Slugger beamed from ear to ear.

"I have to say, I fucking love that . . . way better than fucking Slugger. The weed for me at least is different. If anything, I am more alert and paranoid, which is good. Alcohol makes you too cocky. Too slow . . . too stupid. I, for one, cannot afford that." Carli looked at him and nodded before taking a swig of her claimed moonshine.

"Fair enough," she said as she cleared her throat and wiped her lips.

As the night carried on, Carli cemented her part in the group as an equal. When she had the floor, many listened. "I swear you look like this guy I dated . . . I mean, I was so convinced, but you can't be. He was kind of a pussy. Your face though, it's just . . . I mean, that guy was totally cool, but he really was kind of a pussy." Everyone laughed, including one of the larger gents, whose laughter was boisterous and distinctive. Slugger forced an embarrassed smirk on his face as he studied the flames, and

Carli continued, "Poor guy. He probably died early on. Don't expect much from people like that. All of us . . . we are here because we were born tough . . . even before all this." Carli's crowd cheered in agreement.

"Amen!" Jim yelled, stumbling over himself. Slugger wasn't pleased with that, and his smirk faded as he continued to stare at the fire blankly. Carli looked at him, waiting for a response, as she'd hoped her words would stir him, reveal him.

"Sounds like you ain't really ever had a man." A filthy yet handsome and large man who had recently begun the balding process approached. He used his sweat to slick back the remainder of his hair. Carli looked at him in disgust. Some of the other men snickered.

"Shut the fuck up, Tom!" Jim barked, and Tom sent him a careless middle finger and a wide grin, but his gaze was stuck on Carli.

"I'm just messin', but you're pretty fuckin' funny. You mind if I sit here?" he said, gesturing to the limited space between her and Slugger.

"Umm . . . okay," she said as she scooted over to make more room. As he sat down, Slugger got up and walked away discreetly. Carli noticed, but her attention was drawn back to the grimy man with copper eyes.

Tom was clever, a little more than he let out to be, slipping into the good graces of the war chief while at the same time constantly pushing boundaries and seeking forgiveness. They played a game of testing one another, a game that was enjoyed, for the most part. "So, what's your story? Seems like it'd be an interesting one," he said with charming dimples.

Slugger was taking a long leak in the dark away from the group. When the last drops were shaken off, he remained there, staring off into nothing with an unsure face. His left eye started to twitch faintly, and then it stopped. The crazed man shook his head in subtle refusal, his eyes shut. As he started walking back, everyone was laughing, but one laugh stood out: Carli was cackling hysterically and resting her hand on Tom's shoulder. Slugger stayed back for a moment to observe.

"So, what's his deal?" she asked Tom once the racket and clamor eased.

"I don't know. Slugger's weird . . . kind of fucked up in the head," Tom said, switching his relaxed mood with an anxious and resentful one.

"I guess we all are," Carli asserted.

"Yeah, but not all of us rub our fucking cocks when we kil—"

Steel replaced sound. Interrupting Tom's sentence was a long, serrated knife that went through the back of his head and poked out of his mouth. A scarlet mist splattered Carli, but her reaction was delayed; she stayed silent, watching in horror as Slugger persistently slid the blade in and out, upwardly splitting apart his head. He struggled, but managed to get through the skull while the brains spilled all over him. He then kicked the corpse into the pyre and sat down next to the saucer-eyed girl of his dreams. The rest of his men looked down, continuing their dining and drinking in awkward silence while a few walked away, annoyed.

"You wanna know what I whispered to your little faggot friend?" he asked Carli, his eyes blackened and a cruel twisting lip on his bloody face. She glared into his tattered soul, refusing to look away. "I told him if he flinched or passed out early, my boys would run a train on you. You're right, that little guy turned out to be a true badass and held up his end. Just want you to know, Tom was kind of on the rapey side. So, who knows . . . I might have just done you a favor. But why don't we just sit back and enjoy the show for now?" Slugger leaned back and stretched out his legs, folded his arms, and cuffed the back of his head. He took a deep breath, inhaling the fumes and relishing the sound of burning flesh and clothing.

Carli spat spitefully on the ground before she got up and walked away, tasting blood that wasn't hers. She found her claimed spot, and the tall grass called her name. Slugger had gifted her a sleeping bag before the drinking began; it had no cushioning and felt like a wet space blanket, but it was enough. The drink wrung her insides and pulled her eyelids shut like window shades. A teardrop fell, and she wasn't sure whether it was for the dead or the living; it took her a lingering moment to find his name, but her lips could only form the word "Slugger."

The sun poked its orange mane above the skyline. "Get up, sunshines!" Jim yelled. "I wanna get home before dark!"

The men got up grudgingly and packed the vehicles with resentful haste. Carli awoke groggily. She tried to brush through her matted hair with her fingers, then rolled the sleeping bag up and packed it away in one of the trucks amidst the scuffling of the others.

"I wanna apologize for last night," said Slugger from behind. She turned to greet him with a daggerlike scowl. "Come and ride with me," he said, kind, yet still in a way she could not refuse.

As she waited in the passenger seat, Slugger fastened the muzzle on Homer using an extended pole of oxidized umber metal, hooked at the end. He then put it away in the trunk of the convertible. Homer shook his head truculently once the muzzle was securely locked on, riling up his female counterpart.

"Hey! Marge, what the fuck? Here." Slugger took out a

human foot from the trunk before he closed it and tossed it at the female dragon. The cold clammy trotter hit her face and dropped to the floor, which she responded to by licking it up and swallowing it whole. "I fucking love her," Slugger whispered to Carli as he started to mush his reptilian reindeer.

"Hold up! Boss!" A man with a scar-crossed eye and a shower of long black dreadlocks exited the shade with a hostage. It was a hungry young man, unarmed. Slugger jumped out of the vehicle and blustered toward the prisoner with a smile. "He had this." Slugger's soldier handed him a backpack, which he looked through.

"Pretty light. You by yourself?" he inquired.

"Yes," the man said, trembling.

Slugger widened his smile. "How long have you been following us?"

"I'm not following anybody," the man said defiantly.

Slugger dwelled on his face, analyzing every detail for an excruciating moment. ". . . Well, I can't just let you starve out there." He walked over to a crate ready to be loaded and revealed a small sack full of candy-colored and oddly shaped edibles. "Here you are, my friend. This land is ours . . . just don't cause any trouble," Slugger said with a wink. He then turned around and got back into his vehicle.

The dreadlocked guard pushed the lone man away. "Get the fuck out of here!"

The young man ran off down the road in the opposite direction, gripping the gifted sack as it swung with his stride. The dreaded man with the scar approached his commander. "Those were mine," the henchman stated brashly. Slugger eyed him, though his sight seemed vacant.

"I'll personally get you more, you big fucking baby. Now

follow him and find out where he stays." With no other sign of acknowledgement, the man gathered a scouting party and headed out into the woods.

"What . . . you gonna give him a foot too?" Carli quipped with her sandy charm.

"Ha!" Slugger laughed out loud, and felt that that alone would suffice as an answer. He mushed his beasts forward and the rest of the caravan followed.

Chapter VII – The Lost Boys

On the road, Shane and Bastian stumbled upon a muddy jeep with broken mirrors. "You know how to hot-wire a car?" Shane asked, examining the abandoned vehicle.

"Nope," Bastian said with a cocksure grin while twirling a set of keys around his index finger. Shane glanced over, lifting his brows with both shock and relief. He sat in the passenger seat and Bastian fiddled with the keys to find the right one. The car stubbornly started, and they took off trailing black smog.

As they drove down the road, Shane regularly glanced behind them to make sure they weren't being followed. Bastian was able to anticipate his pivots as if they were on cue.

"We good?" he jested with eyes glued to the road ahead.

". . . Yeah," Shane relayed, unmindful of the jab.

"How are we going to find that spot?" the mountainous man then asked.

"Not sure, but at least we know we are heading in the right direction. Still, knowing Carli . . . she's not there anymore. I wouldn't be," Shane reminded him.

"I know she's not, but it's a start," Bastian replied, and his longtime friend nodded in agreement.

"One thing I do know is that she's alive," Shane assured Bastian with beads of sweat falling from his temples.

"That's for . . ."

Their moment was interrupted by the buzz of engines echoing in the distance. The sounds became more apparent, gradually growing louder from behind. Shane and Bastian looked at each other, reassuring themselves that it wasn't just the noises in their heads. "Gas it!" Shane commanded. Bastian obliged, but the roars from behind just grew louder. Shane turned around and saw motorcycles barreling down the road toward them. "Looks like it's only two," he claimed.

"Let's hope so." The car suddenly growled, sputtered, and began slowing. "What the fuck!" Bastian panicked.

"It says the gas is full!" Shane exclaimed.

"The gauge hasn't moved since we left," Bastian spat as he punched the faulty dashboard, drawing cracks on the glass and plastic. The jeep then rolled to a complete stop. The motorcyclists were catching up and began hailing bullets their way that perforated the back of the jeep and one of the tires. The jeep sank lower on its right side.

"This is the last one," Bastian said as they ducked and crouched low. He pulled a pin out of another grenade and tossed it toward the motorcycles. The explosion went off and a cloud of smoke and flame blanketed the assailants. One bike tumbled and rolled without its rider while the other sped through the firestorm. However, the driver was disoriented and regaining his vision, and he approached the vehicle too abruptly. Shane threw his door open with perfect timing and the rider was tossed from his bike, taking the door with him. The hinges on the jeep clinked and wailed, and the door skidded forward, shaving the top layer off the ground.

"Nice," Bastian commended as he gave a sigh of relief. The sweat on his brow felt cold against the wind.

Shane rushed toward the man now lying in the dusty gravel and slit his throat. He didn't know if the man had survived the crash, but he killed any doubt with him. He turned to face Bastian. "The other one . . . make sure. We have to get out of here now."

The sun vanished and the moon, almost full, greeted the night with its violet incandescence. Dinner was a pair of blue fruits they found hanging low from a dwarf tree. They were similar to a papaya, but slimmer and lengthier. As the juicy flesh watered their mouths, the two trudged on. They trailed off the road, following the North Star, still white and unchanged.

"We have to rest . . . gotta set up camp," Bastian panted like a broken vacuum. Shane looked up at the moon and back out into the distance.

"I don't think we should sleep until tomorrow night. There's so much light out, we can't just leave it to waste. These borders that man mentioned . . . I want to be sure we pass them; Carli must've by now." Bastian collapsed to the floor and rested against the pale trunk of a wilting sequoia-like giant; the once golden leaves had dried to silver, and the reddish vines were cracked and brown. His ribs constantly reminded him of his recent beating.

"Just for fifteen minutes or so," he touted before Shane joined him.

"He said she'd be somebody else's problem? That's what he said to you, right?" the amputee pondered.

"Don't think too long on the words of a miserable drunk . . ." Bastian suggested, somewhat uncertain. Shane remained silent, contemplating their next move.

"Alright, let's go," he eventually said, springing back up to his feet.

"That wasn't even five," Bastian moaned.

As they walked through the night, the woods grew denser and they found themselves struggling between gargantuan wooden columns that blocked the moon's luster. Still, they managed to get through by finding open patches in the canopy and following the sky's compass. Dawn approached and the stars faded away with the invading light. Both men were melting with exhaustion.

"We shouldn't have done that," Bastian said. "Now today is going to be that much harder," he added.

"Oh come on, it's not like we haven't done this before," Shane said with saintly optimism and a smile as he brushed aside his fatigue.

"Now I know what Carli was talking about; Leonard too, actually," Bastian scoffed as the iron taste of blood leaked into his air sacs.

". . . What?" Shane inquired, dropping his grin.

"They both said, in their own ways, that you have this unnatural and sometimes annoying way of never getting tired and pretending to be happy about it in some attempt to inspire us."

Shane took in the statement for a moment and responded with a humble smirk.

Eventually, they came upon a maze of honey grass with blades taller than men. The sound of rushing water murmured on the other side, the sweet lullaby of spring. Still, the cycle of seasons once known was no longer promised with the climates of Earth forever changed. This spring had run long, while others had seemed short. Fall always happened, but winter did not; not since the Dark Winter. Those left to wander and scavenge were lost in time, and little did they know it had been eleven years;

eleven years since the fall of society, and eight years since the black clouds and black snow had retreated and unveiled a new world. Today, the water was music, and so was the air; the song of spring continued on.

"I can't see shit, can you?" Shane asked, pushing aside the yellow swords towering over him.

"No, but I think it's getting louder," Bastian responded, feeling small for a change.

Finally, the curtains revealed a steady stream courted with waist-high palm trees at its edges. Many of the trees were stout and looked like they were ready to burst through their bark; others were twisted hideously with blistering mutations and deformities. The altered specimens bloomed golden bananas; some spotted brown, others black as night.

"What in the hell did they do to our world?" Shane wondered aloud. Bastian heard a disturbance in the water and glanced over. He noticed a round blob of fur at the edge lapping up water from the babbling brook. Bastian tapped Shane and motioned him to remain silent so as not to spook their possible prey. They each took out their hunting knives and crept toward the animal through the grass, almost blindly. The penetrating sound of a bird whistled through the air, yet was ignored. The paunchy creature up ahead had matted black fur and dragged its gut through the mud on all fours. It had a thick rounded tail that sporadically slapped the ground like a beaver with a twitch. It was mammalian, with a wide mouth, flat head, and short teeth. The creature proudly wore a spiraled horn reminiscent of a unicorn's. The bird whistled again, and Shane looked around, concerned.

"It's just a bird," Bastian whispered, creeping toward the unsuspecting victim, hunger stricken. As he narrowed the gap, a spear was chucked from behind the animal. It pierced through its neck, pinning it to the ground as it dropped lifelessly. Bastian and Shane froze, motionless for a bleeding moment. The bird whistle boomed from behind them once again, and then another responded, closer to the creature.

"We know you're there . . ." a high voice squawked over the air. Bastian and Shane looked at each other, unsure of what to do, choosing to remain silent and still. "Are you gonna make us come get you, 'cuz we will," the voice persisted. Shane stood up and walked through the grass toward the spear-thrower with his arms up in an unthreatening manner, hands just barely visible.

As he approached the creek and revealed himself, Shane began to speak. "We are just passing through . . . in peace," he spoke aloud, looking about, unsure where he should direct his voice.

"Tell your big friend to come out!" the voice barked. Bastian came out willingly.

"What are you guys doing?" the voice asked.

"Just. . . passing. . . through," Shane said, frustrated yet calm.

"Is it just you two?" the young interrogator went on.

"No," Bastian answered.

"Are you with Slugger?" the voice continued.

"Yes," Shane insisted abruptly.

"Then you know who we are . . . say our name." Shane hesitated while Bastian looked to him.

"You want me to say all your individual names?" he asked rhetorically in a mocking tone.

"I want you to say *our* name! If you fuckin' don't we are going to end you!"

"Why don't you come out and face us, kid, before you do

that?" Shane scolded.

The voice exited the grassy shroud across the water and revealed himself. He was short and pale; a handsome kid no older than thirteen with dirty blonde hair under his backward baseball cap. He hid behind bright blue eyes and a pickaxe he pretended wasn't heavy.

"You threatening us with that, kid?" Bastian smirked wickedly.

"No, I love this thing . . . it goes everywhere with me. We're threatening you with that." The kid pointed behind them, to another around the same age, taller and slimmer with black greasy hair and foggy glasses. In his hands he held an AK-47 with a blackened coal-like barrel and polished handguards of glistening wood. A third revealed himself: a fat round kid, seemingly older, with red hair and freckles. He stood by the talkative blonde and wore a white T-shirt that was a size too small and wielded twin machetes, thirsty as they were shiny.

Two other filth-ridden kids with identical faces and wet, tangled chocolate hair appeared and began to drag away the downed beast with the lovely horn. They were accompanied by a shaggy coyote that ran excited circles around them, splashing in the mossy bank. The three disappeared with their catch, unconcerned with the situation at hand.

A sixth and final kid decided to leave their cover, but kept a hand cannon aimed at the intruders. It was white with silver and flared with a rosewood grip. A thick beanie held back hair, and a black bandana veiled a hard face from the nose down. The kid was overly dressed, with winter gloves and an oversized jacket; only a pair of brown expressionless eyes could be seen through a slit in the wear. Shane drilled into the kid's gaze for a sustained moment while their eyes locked. The two men met an angry, young face at every turn, encircled by a pack.

"I'd say it's a fair threat now . . . so, say our name," the blonde demanded.

"We don't know who the fuck you are," Bastian exclaimed. Shane kept his eyes on the piercing brown pools of the masked one.

"We are the Lost Boys, and anyone in Slugger's camp would have known that," the young leader said flatly.

"What the fuck are you looking at!" the ginger boy blasted at Shane, who turned to face the fiery delinquent.

"Who is Slugger?" Shane inquired softly.

"Right now, I'd be more focused on who we are," the baseball-capped kid retorted.

"What can we do for you?" Shane asked.

"There's nothing we can't do for ourselves," the leader said.

"So, you're going to kill us then?" Shane asked with a pinched face.

"Probably, after we take your stuff," the leader answered, prompting the one with glasses and the rifle to chuckle under his breath while keeping a steady aim.

Shane glanced at each of his captors and began to think fondly and bitterly of his childhood. There were pieces he couldn't recall and faces he did not remember. Still, he had once been a child; could they say the same? The brown eyes stuck with him, and he could see them even as he looked away. ". . . The Lost Boys, huh?" Shane asked.

"That's right," the leader insisted.

"Funny 'cuz . . . one of you is a girl."

The kids stood silent, especially the leader. The round red ruffian took a few threatening steps forward. The figure in the fabric guise took off the beanie and pulled down the bandana;

76

she then rested her gun in its holster.

"You got a good eye," the young girl was tan, with smooth olive skin and long black hair that dropped like a dark angel's. "Billy, scout ahead . . . we can handle this," she said to her zealous decoy. He immediately scuffled off to do as he was told, dragging his pickaxe through the grass.

"So, you're in charge?" Shane grew solemn as he asked, though she humbly left his question in the air.

"I want to know more about you," she stated plainly. "We are going to take everything you have . . . that's a given. But we don't have to kill you . . . if you play nice. So, don't give us a reason to."

"They can't live!" the ginger boy bellowed from across the creek.

"Agreed," the scrawny one with the AK said.

"If they make even the slightest move, you boys can have at it, but only if. We have to take them to Slugger," she explained.

"They know you're a girl . . . these two'll tell the other men when we get there," the large boy whined.

"Rudy . . . it's my call," she reminded him sternly. Rudy remained quiet thereafter.

The young ones led Bastian and Shane through the wilderness with barrels pressed to their backs. They eventually came upon a cabin weathered by the fast pace of time that had planks of wood missing from the roof and walls. It was small, but it held an aura of mystery and intrigue, like an old book with a thousand stories. Slouching, it was supported by a gargantuan tree, different from those that surrounded it. The bark was blue and silver with holes and splintered scars. The branches were not pointed and sharp, but rather rounded and curved.

When they got inside the cabin, there was a pig corpse

hanging from a hook. It was shaved, skinned, beheaded, and bled, and the intestines had been cleanly removed. The cabin reeked with a dank odor that made the atmosphere so heavy that Shane and Bastian had to squint their eyes. They crept up to a cellar door that had an extensive web of chains guarding it with slits wide enough in the jambs for the padlocks to slip through, allowing the dwellers to lock and unlock them from both sides of the door. Rudy unlocked them all, each with a different key, until finally the chains loosened their grip. The large freckled boy flung the door open and the chains chirped, chimed, and rattled against the wood; he then vanished down into the black hole.

"After you . . ." the young leader insisted while motioning to Shane. Shane stuck his head through, then slipped down into the cellar. There were no stairs, but a makeshift ramp that looped several times before throwing him into a pile of mulch. As he lifted his head to look around, Bastian launched off the slide and blindsided him into the pile. Leaves, fronds, and twigs were kicked upward as the two struggled in their tangle.

". . . Sorry," Bastian murmured. Rudy roared with ridicule, watching the two indignantly climb to their feet. A rope was thrown down the ramp and the leader climbed down while her thin guard stayed back to relock their precious entrance. "Didn't want to tell us about the rope?" Bastian asked with resentment.

"Where's the fun in that?" she said with a sly wink. Billy the blonde appeared from down a tunnel with a lit lantern and a handgun.

"Talia?" he asked while the flickering flame made their shadows dance.

"We got some new best friends for the night," the young leader announced. "Tomorrow . . . we'll take them down to meet the man."

They led Bastian and Shane down a candlelit passageway that brought them to a den; a hub that connected the vast underground tunnel network. Furnished with collectibles, it was homely, with a rack of knives and spears along one wall and a shelf full of books and comics from the previous era on the opposite wall. The floor was decorated with colorful rugs that framed faces of superheroes and shadows of dinosaurs. The two were amazed by the sight. It was small and simple, but comforting. Sitting on the centerpiece couch was Rudy, the muscle.

"Welcome to our little crib . . . isn't it just perfect?" Talia, the leader of the Lost Boys, opened her arms, presenting their humble abode. Billy joined the other boy on the couch while the scrawny one with the AK managed to catch up, quiet and unnoticed. He homed in on Bastian like a hawk once more and denied him any comfort or room to breathe, almost brushing the gun against him.

"Ease up, kid," the large man turned to warn him.

"Louis is your new shadow. He's good at that. He won't sleep, eat, or talk until he feels safe; until we feel safe. I love it, 'cuz it allows the rest of us to settle down for nice moments like this. So, sit down and tell us something," Talia charmingly demanded as she sat between Billy and Rudy on the beaten couch. Shane sat down in a rickety chair already facing them. It creaked painfully under his weight.

"I guess I'll just stand," Bastian remarked in a salty tone. The boy behind him lifted the barrel, ready to send Bastian's head to oblivion. He then kicked a stool toward the large man, and it rolled and crashed into his shins. Bastian lifted his eyebrows, impressed at the boy's vigor. He propped the stool upright and took a seat without objection. Secretly, the boys gleefully anticipated the stool giving in at any moment from his mass.

"What do you want to know?" Shane asked.

"How about how you lost half your fuckin' arm, to start?" Talia said with a wicked grin.

Shane lifted his head and gazed off in remembrance, then looked back down to meet eyes with his host. "Something big came at me . . . ripped it off, and a group of men killed it before it killed me," he said straightforwardly.

"Your men?" Talia leaned in.

"No . . . these guys had trucks, guns . . . outposts. They were well-organized, and we just happened to cross paths."

"Go on . . ." Talia ordered.

"They thought he was dead and beat me nearly to death," Bastian added.

". . . What did they take?" Talia's smile slowly faded.

"What do you mean?" Bastian asked, failing to mask his disdain. Shane looked to his friend, noticing as of late the shortening fuse of the once patient and soft-spoken giant.

"They always take something . . . so, what was it?" she persisted.

"Our friend, Carli," Shane stated numbly.

". . . I see." Talia said, looking away, and for a moment there was a mournful silence. "The world out there is dead. People want to pretend and deny, string it up like a corpse puppet with pretty clothes and shiny jewelry and perfume, telling themselves the bloodstains are gone and the stench isn't so bad. There's always a reason, always a justification . . . always a fear . . ." she added while the others stirred, confused by her sudden rant and the words she had chosen. "I want you to know this is the best we can do. No matter how much we start to feel for you guys, our guard will not be dropped. We will kill you . . . fast and to the point. We have guns. It won't be that hard for us this time," Talia coldly stated, bouncing her eyes back and forth from Bastian to Shane.

"We understand," Shane said compassionately.

"You do, huh? Then tell me, what is the worst thing you guys have ever done?" she inquired. Bastian remained silent, drowning in his own recall.

"There were six of us at the start," Shane began reluctantly. "The storms were too wild; we were holed up underground in our neighbor's shelter." The kids leaned in to listen, captivated already. ". . . We heard the wind throwing everything around outside. We heard lightning strike the Earth like bombs, louder and more immense than any of the nukes that scorched the planet on the first day . . . and we knew . . . we knew there was nothing left out there. Just smolder and ash, hiding the sun for months, maybe years.

"Without days and nights, time was uncertain. We couldn't leave. We rationed the food, but the water was the first to go. Drinking our own piss got old fast. There were many days and weeks—presumably, of course, we couldn't keep track—that passed without a single word to each other . . . until one of our comrades started to unravel. He started yelling about leaving, and even tried to take our remaining supplies. His reasoning was that if we were going to stay there and starve to death, why not give him our stuff so he could have a better chance outside. After we denied him, he spent all his energy whining and swinging his fists until he eventually passed out. We thought he was gonna wake up, but he didn't. After a while I put my head to his chest and heard nothing.

"Yeah, we discussed it for a moment or two, but we were just deliberating. We all knew the only thing that was going to allow us to survive . . . So, we ate him, and split his possessions amongst the rest of us . . . like thieves, stealing everything he had left in this world right down to the flesh off his bone. Like savages . . . like vermin," Shane loathsomely spat and looked down to the dark, damp floor, seeing a past face drawn in the lines in the dirt.

"You know . . . we ate a guy before, too," Talia related. "He was by himself, polishing his gun, kicking his feet in the water like he didn't have a care in the world. We had no reason to believe he was a threat, but . . . adapting to this world so quick wasn't so easy. I came up from behind and stabbed him in the neck . . . before I knew him . . . before I heard him say anything . . . before I looked into his eyes. We took everything he had and dragged him naked to this cabin. Cutting him up was messy, and cooking him was downright tedious. We ate him, and even enjoyed ourselves . . . making jokes out of his corpse . . . it took a while for that to really sink in," Talia said, glancing at Shane with gloom and age that would not normally occupy such youth. "It's not good or bad, weak or strong. It's about how mad the world is gonna make you." She paused before speaking again. "I hate to do this to you guys, but I'm gonna have to ask you to get in that cage down there," Talia demanded while directing their attention to another tunnel.

"You gotta be . . ." Bastian began, but was interrupted by his level-headed friend.

"We will but . . . if it's okay, we would like to hold on to our knives."

"Why not? Louis is going to be right outside your cage with his lovely AK . . . I did tell you guys he doesn't sleep, right?

He's a fuckin' machine." The girl brightened, seemingly putting aside all of what she had just felt. "Anyway, night." On that note, Talia stood up and walked confidently down the opposite tunnel. Her silhouette was quickly swallowed by a black abyss.

"Come on guys, I think Louis really wants to shoot you," Billy said amiably. As Shane and Bastian stood, Rudy rose as well, scowling at the two. Rudy's stature matched Shane's, and with his new handicap the young boy could easily overpower him, and Shane knew it. Louis jabbed Bastian in the back with the rifle's tip in the direction of the tunnel Talia had pointed at. Although it hurt, he acted as if he did not notice and complied lazily with the implied order. The boys led them to a wooden cage with a crude padlock dangling from the entry latch. Bastian and Shane looked at each other in comic disbelief.

"You sure this will keep us in?" Bastian sarcastically asked.

"Just get in!" the large freckled boy barked. As he petulantly opened the door, he tossed two bananas in the cage for the prisoners.

"Thanks, kid," Bastian sincerely muttered. The Lost Boys secured the coop and turned, refusing to acknowledge the gratitude, and exited the slender tunnel without looking back. "Are they serious?" Bastian asked.

"Let's just try to earn their trust," Shane said, contemplating, always contemplating. "They want to take us to this man . . . anybody protecting a group of children can't be that bad. We stumbled upon people again; organized and resourceful people. These two groups have been here this whole time, while we wandered for years, alone. Maybe they'll take us in, want us to contribute . . . maybe they'll have Carli," Shane thought aloud. Bastian responded with a look that was half distaste and half curiosity. "If they have her . . . we'll get her. If not, we look for any sign and bail," Shane ended abruptly, and Bastian tilted his head.

"How do you know it's not the same group who took her in the first place?" the hulking man inquired harshly.

". . . I just have a feeling. We killed a good amount of their men and sent them scrambling to figure out what the hell hit 'em. The rest would be alarmed or alerted by now. These kids have no clue what we did, and it seems like they're the eyes and ears around here. Let's ride this out, see where it takes us," Shane finished.

"Alright, Shane the restless. But let's not get carried away with hope and have it cripple us any more than we already are. And one more thing . . . we were never alone," Bastian remarked quietly, yet clearly.

Bastian awoke to a bark and a growl. Shane was already awake. Outside the cage stood Talia with the twins by her side. The leader was covered in her disguise again. The coyote blocked the cage door and continued to growl.

"This is Scooby. He's all bark though, trust me," Talia said. "But we aren't," she added with a wink. Each twin illuminated the tunnel with a torch, and the flames reflected off the silver of their handguns. "Before we set off, we need to go over a few things," Talia remarked before turning around and exiting the tunnel. The twins led them back to the den to meet up with the rest of the crew. Scooby ran around frantically barking before finally being shushed by Rudy. There was a crumpled, worn map on a table in the center. "Tell us where you think you were when you were attacked," Talia requested.

Shane walked up and looked at the map intensely while Louis cocked his rifle. Shane ignored the obvious threat. "I don't know, I need a start." He was lost without a reference point.

Talia circled a specific area on the old paper. "This is where we are right now . . ." She then drew a short line southwest of the first circle. ". . . we tracked you guys from here." Shane and Bastian quickly glanced at each other, awed as well as shamefaced.

"We were on a road going north for a while . . . before we got off around there, that makes sense," Shane said, scanning the now discernible map.

"This is the only likely road that you guys would have taken. How long did you travel after you were attacked?" she inquired.

"Days . . ." Bastian butted in.

"How many guys?" Talia asked, this time facing Bastian.

"Six or seven, including their leader, the big, loud, red-headed mother fucker . . . not you," Bastian said, turning to acknowledge the nearby ginger with similar traits; Rudy responded with a grimace.

"That's Cliff . . . he's a real asshole with a whole lot of firepower," Talia informed them.

"But Slugger ain't scared of him!" one of the twins barked.

"Fuck no he's not," Billy added with a smirk.

"We aren't supposed to go over there, and they aren't supposed to come over here." Talia drew a line on the map with her finger. "That's the border . . . if they took your friend, she's gone," Talia said with modest remorse.

"She escaped, and we have reason to believe she went north," Shane clarified. There was silence in the air for a moment, excluding the panting of Scooby the coyote. "So, who is this man you're taking us to?" Shane demanded quietly. Talia stared off for a moment, then looked at Shane.

"When we found this little place, we were so happy. We had so many ideas. We built it with blood and sweat. Hadn't seen people at that point since almost the start . . . since those charged to watch us abandoned us. We were even smaller then . . . playing in the creek, thinking that this world was in our hands . . . that it was ours. Five men, I think it was, surrounded us. One of them jumped in the water after me; he tackled me and held me under. Then he started to take my clothes off while I was drowning. I wanted nothing more than to die right then and there, anything for it all to stop . . . and then it did.

"I remember hearing shots fire, and then blood. I was grabbed out of the lake and remember throwing up so much water and . . . other things. Then I saw him . . . and what he'd done. He killed all those men—his own men—to save us. He told me it was his world, but he can't always protect me from it. He told us that . . . if we wanted to live, we would have to earn it. He gave us his rifle, which is the one your shadow Louis over there is so fond of. He told me to hide my face and cover up before we went back with him. He showed us a fortress with an army of men and monsters helping them live. We wandered around unbothered while he told his men some crazy bullshit story about how we ambushed him and took out his crew. He made us a legend and put us in charge of this sector. That's who he is . . . order amongst the chaos."

Chapter VIII – War Path

Slugger's caravan drove throughout the morning while Carli refused to say a word. The day started to get hot and the trees began to thin out. Along the road, the forest diminished, and all plant life faded and failed. The ground was cracked, and the sky was vast and open. The caravan crossed the outskirts of the wilderness and entered a barren wasteland. They passed the desolate husk of what once was an alpha predator, a great sand millipede, both prehistoric and alien. The road stretched farther than the eye could reach. Carli began to sweat and feel dizzy. Slugger noticed and handed her a canteen of water.

"We're almost there," he assured her. Finally, on the horizon, she could see a wide canyon. Carli took another sip of water before she stood up in the car to get a better view. It took them around fifteen minutes to reach the canyon. Every second it grew larger, and what Carli witnessed astounded her. An extensive byzantine settlement formed from stone, wood, and metal loomed over them.

The settlement filled the gorge and climbed the rocky walls with manmade steps and carved paths, and guard towers and battlements connected the many levels. An elaborate drawbridge started winding open as they approached. The gates were edged with filed railheads, each prizing a skull; and not only human skulls, but also the skulls of various beasts. The drawbridge slammed down on the already-broken ground and a giant stepped out to greet them.

He was the biggest man Carli had ever seen. He had long, stringy black hair that nearly covered his eyes, with spots of veiny white barely visible through the drooping black wire. He wore no shirt but scars and stitches and a hideous burn on his chest that left his skin yellow and purple. On his wrists were shackles, but the chains were broken and, like his arms, swinging free. The caravan stopped outside the gate to unload. The giant walked around Slugger's snarling beasts, unmoved, and straight to him.

"How'd the place hold up while I was gone?" Slugger gave him a crooked smile. The giant remained ominously silent. ". . . Attaboy. This is Carli. Can you help her with her shit up to the room?"

The giant again chose to be silent, his lips straight like a flatline. "This is Ben. He's a real talker, so try not to tell him any deep dark secrets. Get your stuff and follow him. I got a lot of shit to do today, but I'd like to have dinner with you tonight . . . if you're up for it." Slugger parted as the final word left his mouth, not giving her a chance to answer.

Big Ben carried her backpack while she followed him through the stronghold. At the center of it all was a lush oasis full of effervescent life, aside from a dead willow tree standing in the water. Warthogs, rainbow birds, and giant bats shared the watering hole with the men who came and went, filling their buckets without disturbing the wildlife. There was respect and a peaceful omniscience about this natural shrine. Carli observed in awe. Beyond it began the maze of roofless corridors and natural alleyways, made efficient by the tools of men. There was a blacksmith striking a hot sword in a cave by the junction of two paths and an auction happening just above on the second level. The place seemed endless.

Further on, there was an open flat area where men were trading goods and had stands and marquees set up. She passed by two separate chop shops, both spewing yellow, scintillating swarf while crews cut into vehicles and hardware. There was a deep kennel that held more than just dogs and foul odors, an empty boxing ring that listed its schedule of bouts on a sign just outside, and a man playing a guitar on a humble little stage where none save a few paid any attention. Above all, in the highest quantity, was movement and sound. And beyond the open area, she saw more areas blocked off, with more men constructing additional expansions. They were like ants with a single mission, and the canyon ran deep.

They finally came upon a lonely tower built into the edge of the canyon. They entered the dark spire and climbed a narrow stair path that led them to the summit. The pinnacle had a provisional balcony that skewed downward, and the floor below had a bedroom. The room had an impenetrable solid steel door, and the colossal man used two keys for two locks, one on top of the other. The door stubbornly scraped along the floor as he opened it with ease, despite the immense weight and drag.

"Nuh uh . . . that looks sketch," Carli protested and looked to Big Ben, unsure of whether he was looking back at her or not through his slimy bangs. The eerie giant didn't even breathe at a detectable sound level, and some wondered if he even breathed at all. "We just gonna stand here?" she snapped. The giant refused to make any gestures and persisted to be still like a gargoyle by the entryway. "Can you just get Slugger for me at least?" she asked, relaxing her tone. Ben stood there for a moment, then wandered off to find Slugger, presumably.

Carli unsheathed a blade from the side of her boot and cautiously waded into the dark room. The light from outside peeked through cracks, giving some semblance of illumination. The room was large and held a king-size bed with holes and rips and rusty springs poking out of the failing mattress. On a nightstand next to the bed was a human skull, cleaned and polished; a trophy cradled by a satin pillow. She looked through the shelves and found only clothes, belts, and holsters. She found some rubbing alcohol and a cloth in the nightstand, along with lighters and some dried purple fern leaves in a plastic bag. There was a brown leather trench coat hanging off to the side, massive in size, fit for a great king or lord of the apocalypse. As she searched through its pockets, Slugger entered the room, quiet as a cat.

"Looking through my shit?"

Carli was startled when he decided to speak and reveal himself, but schooled her face before spinning around.

"Maybe," she said sharply. "This your room?"

"Yeah, but it's yours for the night, I got somewhere else to sleep. Did you need something?" he asked impatiently.

"So, am I just supposed to stay here the rest of the day?" she inquired with scorn.

"You can do whatever you want . . . unless it somehow interferes in any way with what we got going on." She looked at him with crossed arms, unsatisfied with the answer. "Just relax and rest for a bit . . . I got some shit I gotta finish up," he said as he exited with haste.

She lay down and looked at the ceiling for roughly an hour, memorizing every crack and bump. Eventually, her distraction put her to sleep, and she became lost in a dreamland.

She woke up with a heavy head and crusty eyes. Her throat tingled with dryness and a succession of coughs could not clear it. Her head throbbed. Looking over, she found a glass of water at the edge of the nightstand next to the skull. It was not previously there, and she shuddered to wonder who came in while she slept. She chugged the water until it was gone and then realized she had to use the restroom. She found a closet with a rustic chamber pot that was luckily emptied. Carli plopped on it hesitantly. As she released her bowels, someone banged on the door. She looked at it, but refused to respond in her state. The banging persisted. "Carli . . . I'm coming in," Slugger drawled from the other side of the door.

"Hold up!" she spat rudely. Slugger waited patiently. When she finished, she moved to the door and struggled to open it. "Jesus Christ, Ben makes this look so fucking easy," she said, huffing and puffing. Slugger chuckled.

"Seriously. . . you get enough sleep?" he asked sarcastically.

"The sun's still out," Carli noted, annoyed and confused at the obvious slight.

"You mean it came back out and now it's about to go back down," Slugger informed her, his smirk widening.

"How long—" she began when the eccentric man before her interjected.

"You were out cold a little over twenty-four hours." Carli's stomach began to roar and bubble. "I could hear that all the way from the gates. How 'bout dinner?" he inquired charmingly.

They sat at a dining room table made from a wooden door that was properly laid out with forks and knives in a room below the bedroom. Candles lit the scene while the sun ceased to breathe outside the window. A large roasted pig sat in the center. They each laid a rag across their laps, acting as napkins. "This place is pretty cool right?" Slugger asked while slicing a piece of the pig off and sticking it on his plate.

"There's nothing to hunt around here, is there?" Carli asked while ignoring his question and getting her own slice of meat.

He looked at her ponderingly. ". . . Barren worms, but you need a team and a good arsenal for one of those. This place is . . . kind of dry." He immediately started shoveling down his meal, and his words at certain syllables spewed minor morsels of pork and dribble. "This is where all the planning and building and trading happens. Welcome to the new capital of the world. Cities, by definition, are apart from nature, right?" he rhetorically asked. "We have an empire, essentially, from snow to sand with thirteen outposts and plans for a mountain fort in the works," Slugger boasted proudly. Carli shrugged and began to eat. "Have you seen anything like it?" he asked.

"Honestly . . . no, this place is something else. You guys are good. I would have never imagined a place like this," she remarked while looking down at her plate.

"Why are you acting like such a fucking pussy right now?" There was a sudden twitch in the warlord's eye and a chilling calm in his voice. She looked up at him, immediately infuriated. "I'm serious. You walked around my men like a fuckin' badass, like you'd bend them over . . . what happened to her? So, I killed two people in front of you . . . and I did enjoy it. Doesn't mean I don't have rational fucking reasons as well. I know you aren't scared, that's not why I'm calling you a pussy. You look at me in hatred and disgust with standards from a world now dead. That . . . is some pussy ass shit," Slugger proclaimed, expressionless, drilling into her with marble eyes. They were concentrated, cool as a light blue flame.

"Tom was one of your own men . . . and Randyll . . . you fucking asshole. He could have helped you, contributed. He was strong and loyal, and that's something that is of value today! What standards? I look at you as a leader, and all I see is stupidity and spite. Someone like you . . . a place like this . . . you're just going to destroy it all in the end, and you know it . . . and you're scared," Carli said fervently while her elbows dug into the mahogany of the table. At the end of her impassioned statement, she pointed at him, and although the distance of the table prevented her from contact, he felt as if she had pressed her finger below his collarbone.

Slugger studied her before responding. "Tom was talking shit about me for weeks and I've let it slide. He wouldn't be the first and he won't be the last . . . but to a stranger, to a newcomer—I cannot let that shit slide. And that kid, Cliff's boy, I already went over that, so think what you want. You might be right, maybe I'll bring it all down upon me . . . and maybe I'll just have to take this whole fuckin' world down with me," Slugger taunted while creeping his smile back into place. "I am scared. There is no shame in that. Your own fear can be a very powerful thing." He cocked his head.

"Scared of Cliff?" Carli inquired softly, poking the bear.

Slugger scoffed. "Me and Cliff respect each other. We are both leaders of men who control vast territories. We are the blueprints of society. Imagine what this could be a hundred years from now," he said as he pounded the table, rattling the dishes.

"Hmm . . . funny . . . you think he feels the same way?" she asked before sipping her water and cutting off a second helping from the pig.

Slugger remained motionless and quiet while she continued

to eat nonchalantly. His blood began to boil. "What are you talking about?" he asked softly, but Carli could sense the nuclear reaction she had just triggered.

"It's just . . ." Carli delayed while she tried to make something up on the spot. "Well, Randyll was telling me about that border you guys honor so dutifully . . . how Cliff's been complaining about it and that they were talking about scouting beyond it. I heard you were scared of him, and that's why you suggested a border in the first place," Carli further instigated.

Slugger looked at the pig and then cut another slice off. "It wasn't even my idea, that fuckin' coward. What kind of pussy lies like that?" he whispered to himself, seemingly relaxed.

"They made it seem like this treaty was just so they could save their ammo. They called your men nothing but animals and you . . . an angry child who calls himself king." The venom dripped off her tongue. They ate in silence. After he finished his third helping, Slugger threw his plate behind him, and it crashed through the window. A few seconds later a faint, pained yell cried out from below, but Slugger and Carli ignored it.

"Where's this coming from, Carli? I mean, I should clearly take you by your word because you have no motive . . . right?" he asked, and Carli could feel the weight of his words. A weak wind forced its way through the window, howling through the jagged opening. Still, she kept her cool.

"My motive is to make you feel like an idiot. You act like there is some respectful, unspoken bond between the two of you. I think it's funny." Her voice was salty ice.

"I could show you something funny if you really want to laugh," Slugger posited with seething malice. It was then Carli knew she had to be careful; his gaze fell upon her like the shadow of an axe.

94

"If only Randyll were here to back me up. I know you remember me, as I remember you, and despite what you were, you could always see someone's intentions . . . someone's fake smile. And me . . . I would never spare anyone's feelings over the truth, not even my own safety. The truth is . . . those men are already lost, already desperate, but you . . . you and your people are not. You will feel their desperation sooner or later, that I can promise. Are you gonna wait to see if I'm right? You know me. Let's put them in check, now. Yes, I want revenge. I want him to pay. I want someone . . . to pay . . . and I think you do too." Carli's cunning desperation was one of her greatest strengths. It had allowed her to get through all manner of situations in the past. She would pair the truth with sparse falsities, blending them in so as to be unrecognizable. For a second, she thought of an old nickname the other girls had given to her at school: "Scorpion," said to have the stinger of a bitch, and in this moment she wielded it again. Slugger studied her with a ponderous look, then stood and kicked his chair back.

"Alright . . . we move out in two days. The red fuck isn't gonna know what hit him!" he bellowed, and Carli responded with a sinister twist of the lip.

The next morning the swaths of the canyon were filled with men and beasts looking up to the warlord's tower, waiting for an announcement. He appeared slowly and dramatically, after some deliberation, from his perch. He carried a megaphone, but before he began, Slugger took a reading of his crowd.

"We . . . are the last men. We get to put back society, and we have been doin' a mighty fine job of that." His men erupted in raucous cheers. ". . . I mean, look at what you guys have built! It's fuckin' awesome! It took a lot of hard work . . . a lot of planning . . . a lot of blood. But look where we are," he said as he opened his arms wide. ". . . And it's only the beginning," he stated and smiled with his obnoxious crowd. "But there's just one thing . . ." he said as the audience hushed. "We tried to be merciful . . . and we all know how fucking hard that is; I want to give you guys props for putting up with Cliff, that piece of shit, that big red faggot! I think he's got a death wish, fucking with us! Now, that never ends well, does it fellas?"

The men roared in outrage that echoed thunderously against the canyon's innards. "He crossed into our lands. We gave them that forest, told those boys to behave, and what do you know . . . they didn't. The morning after tomorrow, we ride out to give 'em a good old fashion spankin'. Meet with your generals after this and they'll tell you your jobs. What do I always tell you, boys? This world . . . it's up for the taking, and they got a nice little arsenal, don't they? So let's take it." His speech had the desired effect. They answered with ground shattering stomps and bloodcurdling cheers and howls.

"Good speech," Carli said from behind him, her arms crossed.

"It was, huh? I'm not sure if they've noticed yet, but I've used the same lines multiple times and it still has the same effect," he said, turning to face her.

"Listen, there's no one who wants to do this more than I do but . . . we gotta talk about one thing that needs to be clear." Carli's voice was prepotent.

"I guess this can be your show. Let's go to my room," he suggested coyly.

After they climbed down the ladder leading to the room below, Slugger sat on the bed while Carli remained standing. "What's up?" he asked.

"Cliff and his men need to die . . . but his wife is there, and she's carrying their unborn child." Her compassion surprised him, and he rubbed his forehead.

". . . Fuuuuck . . . . I wish you didn't tell me that."

She unfolded her arms. "Why?" she demanded.

"Who's going to take care of her? Where's she going to stay? We don't have any real doctors, and we sure as hell never had to deliver a baby before. And if she gets caught in the crossfire . . . well, I can't exactly tell my men not to shoot back."

Carli sat down next to him. "I know we can do this without hurting them."

Slugger stood up and paced the room. "Look, you need to be prepared for the fact that she and the baby may die. It'll probably haunt someone like you. If she's smart, she'll take cover and wait it out. She'll have time . . . me and Cliffy boy gotta chat before the shit goes down anyway. It might not even go down, and we'll jus' end up killing him and the men who touched you." Carli looked doubtfully to the ground. Slugger walked over to her. "I'm sorry for what happened to you, I truly am. I just didn't think you were ready to hear that. But nothing, and no one, will ever touch you again. I will burn this entire world down and swallow the ash before I let even a flake fall upon you."

Carli's eyes began to water, and she looked away. "Why?" she demanded.

"Because . . . I lost you once . . . and that will never happen again," he said softly. Carli looked at him, and they slowly moved in on each other. He brushed her hair behind her ear and left a finger lingering lightly on her lobe. He touched his forehead to hers. Their skin was cold, but the touch was warm. She squeezed his face hard and kissed him tearily. They began to tear wildly at the other's clothes with lips securely locked.

Slugger's shoulder holster dropped to the ground while the Beretta plopped on the hardwood. He nibbled on her bottom lip aggressively while she played with his hair. The two made love throughout the day, and all night, until the break of dawn; until the returning sun soaked into their pores and their sweat glistened.

When they finally finished, Slugger gently grabbed her chin and planted a wet kiss that she was charmed by. After he let go, he jumped off the bed and began to dress. "I got a lot of shit to do today. You're coming with us . . . but you're going to stay in the reserves, so you don't really need to know much. Pack up and be ready to move as soon as you wake up tomorrow." He rushed to the door and had trouble opening the immense slab of steel. "Fuckin' piece of—" He was interrupted by Big Ben, his silent enforcer, who helped him swing the door open with ease from the other side. "Thank you, sir."

Before he exited, Carli objected. "I want to be on the front lines!" she exclaimed.

Slugger rolled his eyes. "There's organization to this . . . I have many crews, each led by a general. They have their own special skills and jobs to do. Me and you . . . we'll be up front so you can watch. But you're gonna get back if bullets fly. We don't have a lot of guns, so we're taking a different route," he told her.

"What about you?" she was curious and slightly apprehensive. Slugger smiled.

"I know Cliff all too well. I know exactly what he's going to pull . . . and I'm ready for it." He left her with her thoughts. Carli stared at nothing in particular and cocked her brow.

* * *

The sun began its descent and brought about a pink sky. Shane, Bastian, and the Lost Boys marched on through the diminishing woods until they approached its terminus.

"We set up camp here," Talia stated while dropping her pack in the dirt and claiming the proximity. "We need to fill up on water before we trek the wastes. We'll make it before dark tomorrow, hopefully. Miles of nothingness . . . with no wheels." She sighed a tepid sigh. "Set up, I'll scout around," Talia ordered as she vanished past the line where forest and desert met; where the last harlequin bramble stood and flagged its colors.

"She kind of reminds me of someone . . ." Bastian said with a smirk and a fixed gaze on Shane, who smiled slightly in acknowledgement. The rest of the crew began to set up without complaint while an overly ecstatic Scooby ran around them, getting in their way from time to time. They erected a fire by nightfall, glowing radiance and visibility. The boys' banter was full of jests, insults, filthy remarks, and half-baked stories and legends. The two men, however, did not feel as high-spirited as their youthful companions. In this world, age would come to one faster and harder than in the previous era of comfort and luxury, and they both knew it to be all too true. In the corner of his senses, Shane felt a presence and stood up, blade in hand. The boys were silenced by his maneuver, and then a rustle in the brush. Talia revealed herself from the shadows with an intrigued smile.

"Can't sneak up on this one," she remarked. Scooby ran to welcome her joyously, springing in the air as if desperate to level with her. She began to playfully tussle with the energetic pup. "What use are you if you can't even sense me coming, huh?" she said to the oblivious coyote.

Bastian rose and walked off to drain himself. Shane sat back down hesitantly, and Talia joined him. "I hope this all goes well . . ." she said. Shane, however, remained silent, staring into the whispering flames. A shriek came from nearby soon after. Everyone stood up, weapons ready.

"Fuckin' A!" Bastian barked as he approached them hastily through branch and thicket. "I got bit!" he barked as he appeared in the fire's light.

"Let me see!" Talia demanded. Bastian took a seat next to her and rolled up his pants. In doing so he smeared the blood, making it unclear where the breach was. Talia poured some water to rinse away the red. There were two puncture wounds in his calf parallel to each other.

"What is it?" he asked.

"You tell me," she responded sharply.

"I don't know, I didn't see anything!" he bellowed.

"Looks like a snake, maybe . . . could be a spider." She examined it. The boys chuckled.

"What's so funny?" he snapped. Talia quickly and accurately cut a bloody X atop the fanged marks before Bastian could even react. The crimson flux increased, and his sock grew cold and drenched. She then stood up with a smile, slid her knife back down her sleeve, and looked to Shane.

"Your friend here is gonna have to suck out the poison . . . in case there is any poison."

Shane looked at Bastian, feeling pistol-whipped.

"What? I'd suck you too, man!" Bastian exclaimed. By that point, the boys could not control their hysterical laughter, but once it ceased, they began to chant in unison.

"Suuuck it . . . suuck it, suck it, suck it, suck it."

Shane shot a glance toward Talia, who shook her head, yet was clearly amused. "Has this actually worked before?" he asked her tiredly. She shrugged, then joined her crew in chanting. Shane grew increasingly aggravated, but as he looked down upon the man who had been there for him longer than he cared to remember, his resentment softened. "You better not tell Carli about this," he said stiffly.

The large man ignored the taunting chants at Shane's expense and responded with a thankful nod. Shane splashed more water on the wound to clear the excess. He then pressed his lips against Bastian's hairy bite and X, siphoning viscous fluids with horrid tastes like an amateur vampire breaking in his curse. The boys erupted in comedic detest.

"Faggot!" Rudy yelled, and their laughter deepened. Shane spat and continued, spat and continued, spat . . . until Talia rested her hand on his shoulder.

"That's probably enough," she stated in a whisper.

Shane stood up with a sudden ferocity and walked slowly toward the ginger bully. Rudy, noticing this attempt at intimidation, stood up and approached the man's wrath. They each came within an inch from the other's face.

"You gonna do something, stumpy?" Rudy inquired with a deep, threatening baritone. Shane drilled into the kid's eyes with his own.

". . . What do you have besides your size and your big fuckin' mouth, huh? You think you can say and do whatever you want . . . to us? I've killed men twice your size with one fuckin' hand, boy. I'll shove my stump up your little dick hole and make you apologize. I'll keep it up there and work you like a puppet until I'm bored . . . until I kill you," Shane spat.

". . . Shane?" Bastian, concerned, stared at his friend in disbelief while Shane refused to look away from his orange target.

"Say something else tubby . . . please, I fucking want you to," Shane persisted. Rudy began to slowly sit back down in submission as the hairs behind his neck pricked up. Louis continued to aim his gun directly at Shane's head, as he had from when the two had initially sparked conflict. It wasn't the words spoken that frightened them, but rather the tone, the pulsating veins, and the black eyes that vowed things far worse than the promises of speech. Bastian put his hand on Shane's, attempting to lower the readied blade. Shane shoved the gesture away, flashing deadly metal. Bastian stood his ground but gazed at him in understanding.

"It's been a while since you've snapped. It was bound to happen again sooner or later, right?" Bastian scolded him with a blank face. Shane seemed different, lost within himself. "We're getting close . . . is that it?" he asked his rage-filled companion.

"Yeah, we're getting close alright." Before he turned around to disappear in the darkness, Shane gave them all an eye; an eye wrought with the foulest of hatred.

". . . Watch out for snakes!" one of the twins reminded him.

"What the hell was that?" Talia spoke for the rest of them.

"He just needs space from time to time," said the giant with a heavy head. He unfolded his pant leg and rolled it down. A slick streak of cold was left where the blood was still trickling down. "He holds it in . . . we've all been through hell, but he tries to smile, he tries to lead with hope. We all saw the cracks get deeper every day. And then, something will trigger him . . . just like that. He'll feel bad in the morning."

Talia seemed uncomfortable. "This is probably not the best time but . . . that trick doesn't work. We were messing with you, cruelly maybe. We'll keep an eye on you tonight; we have things to keep poisons at bay," she said with a guilty conscience.

Bastian though, pretended not to hear her words and instead thought only of his friend; and whether it was due to strength, will, or pure luck, no poison ever hindered him.

Shane and Bastian awoke to the blazing sunlight that cracked through the remaining tree line and bleached the vast wasteland up ahead. Bastian blinked and rubbed his eyes while Shane scanned their camp and noticed only Billy and Rudy. They were sitting on a white log that looked like a giant bone eating thin slices of meat and pig's feet from a jar full of water, browned sugar, and salt.

"You guys want any?" Billy asked cheerily. Shane nodded and walked over to join them.

"Where's the rest of you?" he asked, cloudy and concerned.

"They went to fill up on water and shit," Rudy answered sharply.

Shane looked at him and had to pause for a moment before he could respond. "I'm sorry kid . . . it had nothing to do with you," he said, feeling ashamed after sleeping off last night's mental snap. Rudy silently accepted his apology.

"Well isn't that sweet? Let me get some too." Bastian appeared from behind his friend and held out a hand for a sloppy breakfast. Billy gave him a few morsels of brown, dripping flesh. With the stale morning, the four ate in groggy silence until Talia appeared holding a pot and styling herself with a peculiar bandolier. It was tight and slim, and instead of bullets, it carried several filled water bottles.

"Where are the twins?" Billy asked.

"Sent them back with Scoobs to watch over the place . . . have some things for them to do while we're away," she said, hanging her water belt off a low branch. She noticed their breakfast and waited to be served. Rudy handed her two drooling pig's feet;

fat and bulbous and trickling salty juices. She ate them each in a single bite.

"Aren't we losing daylight?" Shane was uneasy. Talia reached for a second helping before she acknowledged him.

"Give me a chance to eat. It's not like I got up early to go fetch a pot of water, boil it, and bring it back fresh or anything like that," she replied bitterly.

Shane looked out toward the incoming desolation and felt they had reached the edge of the world. He wondered how far they'd come. He thought of Carli and Leonard, and even Gus, beyond a barren yet hopeful horizon. "Thank you . . . for everything," he eventually said.

"Yeah, well, don't make me regret it," she snapped back, releasing a modicum of charm. Their modest and peaceful breakfast ran short. Suddenly, a great horn of torturous misery broke the sky. Rudy and Billy looked at Talia with eyes like pale saucers. She shifted on the log to improve her view and looked into the distance with concern. Eventually, from behind the skyline, roared a convoy of around thirty vehicles including an assortment of trucks, cars, vans, and bikes kicking up a storm of dust and havoc. They appeared suddenly and barreled through the desert. At the helm was Slugger's iconic convertible sleigh being dragged along the cracked earth by his two reptilian hellhounds. "It's . . . a war party," Talia muttered uncertainly.

"So, what now?" Bastian asked. Shane looked to Talia for the answer.

"They are headed for the road, which is 'bout a half mile east. War parties don't stop . . . but they'll be back. We keep moving. We get there and we wait," she said, reassuring her group. Talia then simultaneously looked at Shane and Bastian with swaying eyes. "When we get there, keep your eyes to yourselves and don't wander around, just let Billy do all the talking," she said as the witty blonde kid gave them a confident wink. They packed up the campsite and waited for the thundering army to roll by. The ground shook and the yells and howls of deranged men echoed through the world. Like a train, the tail of the convoy eventually whipped into the alien woods.

Chapter IX – The Heart of Darkness

Slugger stood up in his vehicle and fired a flurry of automatic rounds into the air. As he did, one of the wheels hit a large enough rock that the car rattled. He lost his balance and almost fell out, but Carli grabbed him by the shirt and pulled him down on top of her. He hit his forehead on the car door on the way down, and it started to bleed ever so slightly. Slugger smiled wide and their lips sloppily embraced while the blood leaked down her cheek. Homer and Marge continued to lead them down the road, unperturbed, while the war party moved along behind them. They rode under the sun and the heat, with cold in their hearts and fire in their eyes.

Sometime after the light began to fail, they came upon a fork in their path. Awaiting them at the fork was a group of eight men on foot; one of them being the scar-faced henchman whose dark waterfall of dreaded locks were still visible in the dusk. The convoy pulled up and Slugger exited the car to greet them.

"You guys do not waste a second. I fuckin' love it!" their leader said with vicious joy.

"Everybody's in position, Boss," the dreadlocked operative relayed.

"Good, good. Let's move out!" Slugger commanded. As the group of eight dispersed into the woods, Slugger called out to one of them. "Willie!" The scar-faced man spun around, and his black dreads followed him with a slight delay. "Come back here for a second," Slugger ordered, and he walked him over to the trunk of his convertible. Slugger popped it open and pulled out a sack of familiar looking vegetables. "Told you I'd get you back," he said. Willie smiled and received the sack appreciatively. Slugger then slammed the trunk and jumped back in the car. He whipped his pets with the reins, and they mushed. Slugger directed the first half of the convoy down the left side while the end half broke off to the right.

Carli observed curiously. "You're spreading us pretty thin, don't you think?" she remarked.

Slugger grinned eerily. "You're going to love this, trust me," he said while rubbing his erect crotch over his pants. Carli noticed and snarled her lip in utter disgust.

The war party narrowed down on Cliff's castle in the middle of the woods by daybreak. It was a formidable fortification built upon a small military installation. It was constructed from timber and white wood more than metal and concrete, with a watchtower by the grand entrance and a large, rustic double door gate. The wooden gate had text stamped on it that read *"PROPERTY OF US GOVT."* Cliff and eighteen men stood out front awaiting their arrival. As Slugger and his men slowly rolled up, Marge growled grotesquely while Homer shook his muzzle with hungry irritation. Slugger hopped out with a smile, and his men followed.

"What in the holy fuck do you think you're doing boy?" Cliff bellowed with careful annunciation.

"It's good to see you too, Cliff. I'm doing great, how 'bout you?" Slugger antagonized, drunk with pride. Cliff started to breathe heavy, blushing with rage. ". . . Where's the rest of you?" Slugger asked, turning up his palms.

"Oh, they're coming!" one of Cliff's men barked from behind his commander.

Slugger leaned to face him. "That was a rhetorical fucking question there, pal. Your outposts . . . all of 'em . . . are gone from this plane of existence," Slugger said while turning back to face his brutish foe.

"Bull fucking shit!" Cliff remarked.

Slugger scoffed. "Funny thing is, you know I wouldn't lie about that, but I gotta prove it anyway," he said while he walked back to his car. He grabbed a flare gun from the glove box and motioned with his head for Carli to stay by his side. He shot the ball of flame and light into the air and tossed the gun behind him. A few moments passed before his signal was answered. Multiple pillars of smoke began to rise in the surrounding distance.

"Sir! They're burning them . . . all of them!" a man from the watchtower exclaimed. Cliff refused to lift his fiery gaze from the man he now sought to kill, the man he thought he'd dealt with. Slugger seemed a strange menace now, standing before him with unclear motives.

"Bunch of drunks, your men . . . I don't even think you understand how goddamn easy this was. I for one did not expect it to go so well," Slugger said with a smirk.

"Why all of the sudden, you ungrateful little twat?" Cliff snarled.

Slugger shook his head irritably. "Me, ungrateful? Remember her?" Slugger gestured toward Carli, who approached with a glint in her eyes, knowing that her longing for retribution was about to be fulfilled.

Cliff examined her for a moment. ". . . Nope! Who the fuck

is she?" he asserted.

Slugger turned to face her. "He fuckin' remembers you . . . piece of shit," he whispered to her. "Anyway . . . she's the reason we are here, and she's the reason you won't be." He then directed his attention back to the enemy.

"So, what, you're gonna go to war with me? Over some dumb bitch? I almost respected you, son . . . thought you were gonna amount to be a true leader," Cliff said with disdain. Carli flared her fangs unknowingly while Slugger held on to his trademark smile. Cliff started to inch closer to him while his men remained back.

"You sure you wanna do this, boy?" he threatened.

"Wouldn't fuckin' be here if I wasn't," Slugger responded.

Cliff chuckled maniacally, as if he was about to play his trump card. "Alright boys, stay back! Little Sluggy and I made a deal way back. If shit were to ever hit the fan and things got heated again between us, there would be no war. Just me and him, mano y mano!" Cliff announced to his bloodthirsty men, who started to cackle like a choir of hyenas. "But I don't know. He brought his little girlfriend and their big toys. So, what's it gonna be, Sluggy? These men gonna fight your battle for you?" he asked with an ugly and loathsome grin.

"Just wanted to bring the fans," Slugger replied. The men from both factions circled the two, forming a dueling ring. Carli went back to the apocalyptic sleigh while Marge roared in the background and Homer continued to rattle his muzzle.

Cliff unbuckled his gun holster and tossed it off to the side, and one of his men quickly picked it up. Slugger did the same with the holster over his shoulder. He then removed his blade-carrying belt. "This is gonna be fun, little man," Cliff said, elevating his fists in a boxer's stance.

"Yes . . . it will be," Slugger whispered to himself and did the same. Cliff charged first and swung a mighty fist, but Slugger ducked it and came up with a swing of his own that clipped Cliff's nose. As he did this, Slugger rolled back to gain distance from his giant foe, and the circle of spectators widened. Cliff started to bleed, which he responded to with a chuckle while wiping the slick surge with his wrist. The large bearded man then charged again, but Slugger persisted to dance around him, and it was clear he had gone through some training.

"Come on, come to daddy," Cliff taunted. He lunged to grab Slugger, who dove to the ground just in time to escape his clutches. As he landed roughly, he kicked the red behemoth in the ribs with both power and precision. The blade, all but concealed at the tip of his boot, split between the bones; then it pushed, twisted, and pulled, further separating two ribs before it was yanked free. An arching red string of liquid followed the blade's release. Cliff yelled in pain, then punched Slugger in the face, driving him deeper into the dirt. The force stunned Slugger for a moment and Cliff pounded him with two more blows.

Cliff then mounted Slugger and put his hands around his neck. He put immense pressure into the grip and Slugger gasped desperately for air. "You pathetic little fucker . . . I almost feel bad for this," Cliff said while a rush of red came up and colored his teeth. Slugger's head seemed to swell, almost as if it were about to pop like a pea from its pod. Cliff leaned in real close to the pulsating face under him, likely about to utter the triumphant words of a victor. Before he could speak, Slugger hocked a sharp bloody pebble he was hiding under his tongue straight into Cliff's right eye.

Cliff leaned back, relieving pressure off the throttled throat.

Slugger took the opportunity to force his hand into Cliff's gaping mouth and managed to barely grab hold of his curling tongue and uvula, but Cliff chomped down with instinct. Slugger used all his remaining might to tear out muscle and tissue through the man's gripping teeth before Cliff had time to fully react.

Cliff was weakened and dizzied, and his mouth was full of blood. Slugger managed to crawl out from underneath him, leaving the pieces of his enemy he'd torn out in a dark red puddle. He stood up and wobbled as if he were walking for the first time. He struggled, trying to catch his breath, coughing, spitting, and retching; then he fell to the ground, only to get up shortly after. Cliff's sputtering breaths sounded like the cross between an old broken engine and the muffled dying of an animal. He tried to stand but quickly toppled to the blood-soaked earth, then convulsed periodically until he drowned from within.

After recovering, Slugger walked over to Cliff and stomped his face in repeatedly. "Holy fuckin' fuck! I thought I was dead. Ha! You big red faggot! You're redder than I've ever seen you," Slugger barked.

"You cheated, you fuckin' pussy!" the man from the watch-tower yelled from above.

Slugger scoffed. "Come on down here and say that again, bitch. . . . no? Guess we'll be on our way then," he said. Carli looked at him sharply, but was satisfied when he winked at her, and she became certain there was more to come. Cliff's remaining men stood in silence and stared at his leaking corpse while the caravan turned and drove away.

"What's the plan?" Carli asked as they drove off out of sight.

"That's the plan," he replied, pointing to an armored big rig barreling down the road. His caravan pulled over to make way for the truck, then immediately pulled a U-turn to rally behind it.

"What the—" Carli was interrupted by a splash of pungent urine, poured onto her from a bottle. "Are you fucking kidding me?" Carli screamed. Slugger laughed and emptied the remaining liquid onto himself with pleasure. Cliff's boys aimed and fired at the rig as it approached, but they were unable to kill the driver before he broke through their gates. The rig drove to the center of the compound and crashed into a small building. The driver ran out of the truck and into a hail of more enemy bullets. Although he was armored, they penetrated him in a few vulnerable areas. He managed to get the latch door on the trailer open before collapsing. From within, a horde of screaming bats, massive and blind, flooded the sky, and for a moment blocked out the sun. Slugger's troops began to pour a familiar vile fluid onto themselves, then howled like wolves in the wind. Their cries blended seamlessly with the deadly song of the winged swarm. Slugger quickened the charge, and his army pressed the gas.

"Wait! What are you doing? Stop! Let me out, let me out!" Carli yelled while flailing her arms.

Slugger veered his steeds off to the side and motioned his men to continue into battle. "Don't you want this?" he asked.

"I do . . . it's just . . . what about Wendy?" Carli asked with a heavy heart.

"Who?" Slugger demanded.

"What about the baby?" Carli began to shake uncontrollably.

The ongoing foray spiraled into chaos as the approaching army zoomed through the smashed gate. Jim held on to the back of an ATV with a crazed driver. He gripped his chainsaw, spinning and snarling, and managed to hack at a fleeing enemy as they zipped by. The horde of bats descended to begin the blitzkrieg. They avoided Slugger's men because of the urine they had camouflaged themselves with; Cliff's soldiers, however, were torn apart, thrown around, and devoured by hook and fang.

Gunfire ripped through the air and bats began to fall. A muscular soldier with a sturdy helmet and uniform came out from the armory dragging a large-caliber machine gun and puffing on a fat cigar. He first launched a barrage toward his enemies, then struggled to aim the heavy weapon at the swarm above. He sprayed the sky and bats cascaded onto the battlefield until one man came from behind, stabbed him in the back, and twisted the knife until he dropped. The cigar, still stuck between his dying lips, continued to smoke.

"The baby?" Slugger repeated. "More like the fetus. Ask yourself this: Is burning those piles of shits alive—you know, the ones who raped you!—worth a birth not happening? I fuckin' think so. It's not like we are killing an infant, but maybe this kid becomes another Cliff. Maybe he grows up to be another rapist. Or maybe he grows up to be a good person. Who gives a fuck! The point is, these people shouldn't exist anymore . . . not in my world," Slugger said firmly. He had a furrowed brow and a recurring twitch in his eye. Carli looked at him in disappointment.

". . . Your world?" she asked, solemn and bitter. He stared back in silent confusion.

The conflict raged on with the screams of dying men. Suddenly, Molotov cocktails were cast over the walls from various sides of the perimeter, and the compound quickly became an inferno. One of the makeshift bombs hit the watchtower, and a spider of flame crawled up to its pinnacle. Moments later, a sharpshooter jumped out, ablaze.

Through the smoke, Big Ben appeared holding a forty-inch steel mace in one hand and a chain leash in the other; attached was a white gorilla with vampiric fangs and one cycloptic glowing red eye that looked like a ruby made of magma. The creature seemed to fear the giant man, yet pounded the ground at the sight of other foes. Ben released his grip, and the beast was free to rampage. A bat flew in its face, and the creature angrily yanked it from the air and choked it to death. From behind it, a man discharged a shotgun, but only a fraction of the spray tagged the ape's shoulder. The cyclops charged and clobbered him to death before he had time to reload.

"This . . . is all on me. I knew she'd get caught in the middle, but I just needed my revenge that bad. I'm no better than you," Carli stated, shutting her eyes, envisioning the mother and babe's sealed fates.

Slugger squinted his eyes. "Why are you talking like we're the fucking bad guys here, huh?" he asked scornfully.

"Because we are . . . we all are," she said softly. All of a sudden, Wendy's wail carried from the front lines, but was abruptly silenced. Carli stood up instinctually and exited the car, but could not see her in the chaos of the massacre. Slugger followed. Carli's tear ducts overflowed immediately, and she looked at him as she ground her teeth. "You said you'd try . . . they let us walk away peacefully, and you use that opportunity to destroy the whole fucking place! Kill everyone!" she screamed at him. Slugger remained silent, allowing her to finish. "Anything fucking logical about that, you psycho piece of shit?" she persisted.

Slugger rolled his eyes. "Can I go join my friends now?" he

asked, making light of the situation. Carli hesitated, only for a moment, then swung at him as hard as she could across the jaw. He fell flat on his rear and spat a tooth out before getting up and brushing himself off.

"You do all this now, when you wouldn't even stand up for me, or yourself, before?" she inquired coldly. Slugger's blank face broke and he brought about a sinister grin. Who he once was, he had dangled before her; the hope she'd had—it was all nothing but a joke to him. A twinkle Carli had taken as the remnants of her lost lover turned out to be a ruse, one she had imagined. It was surely him, once, but now a spiteful monster stood before her. He lifted his rifle and sent a barrage of bullets at her knees. Carli screamed and collapsed to the mud. Slugger then unleashed the rest of his clip into her and threw the hollow gun at her scattered remains. He walked toward the aftermath of his apparent victory, rubbing his crotch, strangely unaroused. After a few retreating heartbeats, he began to smack himself repeatedly until the skin of his mask itched and burned and bled.

Chapter X – Imposition

Shane and Bastian, led by the Lost Boys, arrived at the gates of the canyon lair. They were tired, travel-stained, and sweat-drenched. As they moved closer to the stronghold, Bastian studied all the various types of skulls piked atop the railheads.

"Who the fuck goes there?" a guard yelled from above, crass and crude.

"The Lost Boys. And we got some possible recruits!" Billy yelled back up. The guard remained silent, but after a few moments the drawbridge unraveled and slammed on the barren floor. A tall and slender man, bronze in tone, welcomed them with a pack of guards behind him. He had a machete sheathed in his belt and sported a pair of slick sunglasses, black as night with a silver *E* carved in the sides.

"Billy my man, how's it been?" he asked.

"Shit's been pretty boring 'til we found these guys," the young kid said, pointing to Shane and Bastian.

". . . You don't say," the man responded while studying the two.

"They seem able, worked well with us on the way over here," Billy stated. The thin man looked back at Billy.

"Come on in, you and your boys have a drink on me," he said with a smile that showcased a row of rotten teeth.

"Not today, Moose. We just came here to drop them off," Billy replied. The man's smile faded, and Shane shot a vexed glance toward Talia. Only her eyes could be seen through her guise, and she stared back at him blankly, standing next to Rudy in silence. "Sorry man, got a lot of shit to do back home, you know how it is," Billy added.

". . . Slugger's not here," Moose said with a low agitated voice.

"Yeeaahh, we saw 'em roll out. Wish we could wait 'til they get back . . . I'm sure it'll be an epic tale, but got some meat to cure and repairs to attend to," Billy said politely.

"Alright then, you boys be safe out there . . . Bones!" he cried out, and an oily man from behind stepped forward. Around his neck hung three bat skulls, laced together by a fine silver chain. "Fetch them some water for the road back." The man hurried past the gate and darted east toward the base of a tower with a black steel door.

"Thanks, Moose." Billy had anxiously anticipated the offer, but hoped not to ask, thinking it would somehow sully his reputation. Talia suddenly jabbed him in the back, and he remembered. "Oh, Moose . . . could we get some salt as well?" he asked, almost timidly. The bronze man's eyes were hidden behind black shades, but his surrounding facial features conveyed his acknowledgement of the request.

"Tell Bones I said to give you a jar. What are their names again?" Moose turned his attention back toward the newcomers.

"Half-arm over here is Shane and the big one is Bastian," Billy answered.

"Alright Shane and Bastian, follow me." The man turned around and led them inside. Shane turned around one last time and met Talia's eyes before the drawbridge came up and blocked their views. "I'm sure they told you 'bout Slugger. He's gonna wanna talk to you guys when he gets back, but 'til then I've got orders to keep fuckers like you cozy," Moose said with a yellow grin.

They walked past the vibrant oasis that served as the focus of the compound. A small bird plumed in rainbow feathers glided above them gracefully and landed on Bastian's shoulder. At a closer glance, it seemed more reptilian, like an ancient pterosaur rather than a common bird. The innocent creature then wrapped its long, ratlike tail securely around his bicep. Shane and Bastian were amazed, and they each started to muster a glimmer of hope from deep within.

They were led to a tent in the outskirts, past all the action, with three sleeping bags rolled up inside, ready for guests. "You guys can set up here for a few days. Tomorrow morning's meal is complimentary, but only tomorrow. Water . . . food . . . whatever you need, you gotta either go and get it yourself or hit the trading floor, but you gotta bring something to the trading floor to trade. You can come and go as you please but remember . . . we have eyes and ears everywhere, and if you wanna challenge that, well . . . you're free to try," Moose informed them, then exited with a baleful wink.

"What do you think?" Bastian asked softly.

"It doesn't make sense . . . how is a place like this possible? They let us keep our weapons and didn't even search us. How do they keep it running if everyone is fending for themselves?" Shane blabbered on ponderously.

"I meant about Carli," Bastian remarked sternly.

"We'll keep an eye out, but we have to gain their trust," Shane said confidently. Bastian shook his head.

"Keep an eye out? We should be looking for her right now,"

he said, heated.

"Stop talking to me like I don't want to find her. We gotta be smart about this, and we cannot be fighting each other right now, or them," Shane said with an icy wisdom about him. Bastian took a deep breath.

"Alright . . . so what's the plan?" he asked, this time with more patience.

"Can't let these people find out we have a motive. We learn as much as we can and blend in, and we try to do it as fast as possible," Shane declared, then began to unroll a sleeping bag one-handedly. Through the night, they took turns keeping watch.

"Rise and shine, freshmen!" Moose shouted from outside. Bastian awoke suddenly, startled. Shane was already awake and staring into the woven fabric of the tent. Moose then threw something, along with two bottles of water, blindly in. "Gotta eat light fellas, too many mouths to feed. I'll be at the gate when you're ready," he said as he went on his way.

"So much for a meal," Bastian said, lacking appreciation as he opened the mangled knapsack. Inside were two sun-dried strips of brown-blue bark, most likely some sort of fruit. Shane bit into the leathery substance without complaint. As they finished, they both exited the tent with the sun rays bearing down upon them and walked toward the gate. The small winged creature took off from the top of the tent and flapped its colorful wings to roost upon Bastian's shoulder once more. The two men looked at each other and chuckled warmly. As they approached Moose and his crew by the gate, the gangly man opened his arms in a welcoming manner.

"Alright, let's get to business. Big guy . . . what can you do?" Moose asked with a stained grin. Bastian raised an eyebrow.

"What do you . . . I don't know . . . a lot," he responded defensively.

"Alright, alright, easy big fella, don't go hulk on me," Moose said with his hands up. "I'm not worried about you fitting in, just wondering if you got a special skill set or anything, like engineer or doctor or fucking scientist . . . I don't know, anything," he added.

"No . . ." Bastian answered plainly.

"That's cool. You're fucking big, that's enough. I am, however, worried about your friend," Moose stated while turning to face Shane. "Half the hands could mean half the man. So, tell me . . . are you some kind of doctor or scientist or some shit?" he inquired seriously.

". . . I was a teacher," Shane said, staring off into the distance. Moose and his men erupted into laughter.

"Yeah? What kind?" he taunted.

"History," Shane responded, proud and unfazed.

"Ha! That's gonna help!" Moose said as he continued laughing. He eventually wiped a tear from his eye and continued, "But, still, I gotta assume it couldn't have just been his big ass keeping you alive out there for so long. So, professor . . . how are you going to contribute?" he then asked as his men shushed their laughter.

"What kinds of jobs are available?" Shane asked.

"For a cripple? Not sure, but maybe you can go talk to Vinny. He's near useless too. Walk down past the water and the alley of yelling idiots and you'll find a slim path that curves right; its lonely, no other path crosses with it. Before the end, you'll see a black door with a white X on it. Go on in and tell 'em Moose sent you. Bastian, I'm gonna show you 'round the gates," Moose said as he put his long arm around the mammoth man, scaring off his new pet, and led him up a stair path that granted access to the multiple levels of the defenses.

Shane walked through crowds of men talking and trading. He saw a blacksmith setting up shop, carrying a bundle of swords and nameless weapons, all crudely forged. Beyond the path was a crew of guys constructing expansions to the already elaborate compound. He eventually turned right and found a lonely door, black with a white X on it, just before the dead end.

Shane eased open the door and crept in hesitantly, closing it behind him. A lantern in the corner lazily kept the darkness at bay. "Vinny . . ." he said across empty space, ". . . Moose sent me."

Suddenly, a jangle of keys rang outside, and one was inserted and twisted into the lock of the door Shane had entered. As it swung open, a man with a bandana around his head accompanied by a well-maintained ponytail strolled in holding a box of supplies. As soon as he saw Shane, he dropped the box, and everything in it cracked and broke. Then he fell to the floor in terror. "Moose sent me!" Shane barked with his hand up.

"Holy fuckin' mother of god. You scared me half to death!" the man on the floor stated. Shane offered his one good hand to help him up.

"Vinny, right? I'm Shane," he said.

"You look half dead yourself," Vinny remarked while picking up scraps and shards and loose tools and putting them back into the dropped box. "So, what can I do for you, Shane?" he asked.

"I need a job," Shane stated plainly.

"Well there isn't one here, so go and tell that asshole I'm handling everything, alright?" Vinny then started to walk down the room toward a desk that sat in front of an old bank vault. It had a gleaming copper face like a giant penny. He put the box down and pulled out a lengthy list from a drawer.

"Why were you so scared?" Shane inquired while walking over to the desk.

"You still here? I'm telling you, there are no jobs here, I'm sorry," he said while scanning the list in his hand.

"What's behind the vault?" Shane asked. Vinny looked up at him, aggravated.

"Shit! Now, leave!" he cried. Shane stood there for a moment, then took a few steps closer to him.

"Okay . . . but I just have one more question," Shane said calmly.

"What?" Vinny yelled, looking up from his desk chair. Shane suddenly grabbed the man by the ponytail and slammed his face into the desk. Once, then twice. Vinny fell to the ground, unconscious. Shane noticed a bolt latch on the door he'd come in through and locked him and his new interrogatee inside the room with the vault.

The man woke up moments later with Shane holding a knife to his throat. "Woah, woah, easy there, fella. I meant no offense," he said, clearly in shock, though he spoke as calmly as he could. "There might be a job—" he started before Shane interrupted him.

"Shut up! You're going to answer my questions. Okay?" Shane asked hotly, steam nearly blowing out of his nostrils with every breath. The frightened man nodded in compliance. "Why were you so scared?" Shane asked.

". . . 'Cuz I thought I locked the door. I'm supposed to always lock it," he answered with a brittle voice.

"Okay, good start. What's behind the vault?" Shane questioned further.

"Canned goods, seeds, gas, weapons. Are you trying to rob us?" Vinny asked, but Shane did not answer.

"Have there been any new people besides me?" he continued.

"I don't know man, I keep to myself mostly, I wouldn't know," Vinny responded genuinely.

"Have you seen a woman?" Shane was hesitant. The other man pondered the question for a moment.

"Why?" he asked. Shane curled his lip.

"It doesn't fucking matter, now does it? Answer."

"Slugger brought a new girl in, took her with him when they went off to fight this other group," he said.

"What did she look like?" Shane asked, a sparkle glittering amidst the flame in his eye.

"Long brown hair. Didn't really see her up close. She seemed pretty," he answered compliantly.

"Was Cliff and his men the other group?" Shane continued to press his hostage.

"Yeah . . . are you one of them?" Vinny cowered.

"No, I hope you guys kill every last one of them."

"Are you really here for a girl?"

"I'm here for a friend . . . and I will get her out of here, even if I have to kill you and everyone else," Shane promised with solemn vengeance.

"And then where will you go? I don't even know how many men Slugger has, but I've seen over a hundred at a time. They are everywhere, always moving; you try anything, and you'll die, slowly," Vinny murmured under the shining threat of razor-edged steel.

"Is that a threat?" Shane asked, pushing the blade slightly into his skin.

"No! It's a warning. I have a 'friend' as well . . . and she is far away from here. But she's safe. Maybe I can help with arrangements for yours," Vinny said.

Shane squinted his eyes in disbelief. "Why are you here and not there, then?"

"Because his people are everywhere. This way I can make sure they don't ever find her," he replied.

"Bullshit! You are desperate and scared and trying to play on my weakness. That was the wrong choice."

"I swear!"

"No! It doesn't make sense," Shane barked back.

"You're right . . . it doesn't. I should be out there with her, but at least I know she's not alone. So you can kill me . . . I hope you and your friend make it out of here. Go west, if you can," Vinny said, inhaling slowly, hoping to gain back some lost dignity.

Suddenly there were two slams on the other side of the door, followed by a man's booming voice. "What's going on in there?"

Shane began to sweat as he looked toward the door. "Let me handle this," Vinny said calmly. Shane had no other choice but to let him go and sheath his knife. Vinny brushed himself off and unlocked the door. Two large men strolled in past him, one bald and with a hatchet and the other carrying a crowbar. They looked at Shane, and the bald one spoke.

"Who the fuck are you?" he growled.

"This is Shane, Moose sent him here to get a job on account of his handicap," Vinny said before Shane could respond.

The bald one looked at Vinny with raised brows. He grabbed a walkie-talkie from his belt and clicked a dial two times to the right.

"Hey Moose. It's Johnny, over," he said over the radio. A moment later Moose responded.

"What can I do for you, Mr. Clean?" Vinny shook his head at the blatant mistrust but remained silent.

"I got a new guy over here with vault boy claiming you sent him over here?" Johnny continued.

"Yup. Hopefully putting the two together can make one full man, over," Moose replied. The two large men looked at each other and nodded.

"Alright Moose, thanks." He put the radio back in his belt.

"What was with all the noise?" Johnny asked, noticing Vinny had a wet cut on the bridge of his nose.

"We were just messin' around, ain't that right?" Vinny answered while delivering a playful punch to Shane's amputation. Shane responded with a strange, agonized grimace.

Johnny looked at the two with disapproval and walked out with his large friend, exiting with the word, "Faggots."

"What's wrong with your arm?" Vinny asked once they were alone again.

"Do you guys have a doctor?" Shane responded.

Vinny shook his head. "Anyone who could help is with the war party. Let me see . . ."

Shane lifted his sleeve and revealed his amputation. The limb was completely black up to his shoulder, and pus-filled sores leaked over old tracks of scabbed blood. "The arm needs to go, ASAP!" Vinny exclaimed. Shane rolled his sleeve back down.

"I have other priorities at the moment," he stated.

"They'll come back . . . they always do. Slugger can be reasonable, but he's very unpredictable. If she's his, no other man will touch her," Vinny assured.

"Carli will never be anyone's," Shane responded, staring off into the lantern's light.

Later that day, Shane sat alone in the tent staring up at the ceiling. The sun began to settle, and Bastian strolled in with a grin. "Look what I've got," he said as he plopped a plump sack by Shane's feet. Inside there were blood-red cactus flowers with sandy yellow feelers sprouting out of their bulbous cores. "Moose says once we make sure all the spikes are off, they're fine to eat, antennas and all. I tried some. It almost tastes like a sour beet wrapped in spinach; definitely an acquired taste." Shane nodded in response, but Bastian noticed he was distracted.

"She was here . . ." Shane then said. Bastian's eyes widened. "She went off with the leader to fight that other group. She probably convinced him to do it. Everyone here seems confident they'll come back . . . like this is a normal occurrence. I have a feeling that Carli isn't a prisoner here," Shane said, not seeing anything before him, lost in thought. Bastian nodded his head, almost in disbelief.

"So, we wait . . . and then what?" he asked.

"Why don't you rest? You'll know what to do when the time is right. I'm just hashing out the details in my head," Shane insisted with a friendly smile, and though well received, it was observably forced.

". . . Alright, Boss," Bastian said cordially.

The two were awakened early by a blasting horn. They exited the tent at the crack of dawn and followed crowds of men rushing to the gates, ready to welcome the arriving caravan. Slugger was at the helm with his microphone. "Cliff is fucking dead! And so are all his men." As he entered, he shouted gloriously over his cheering audience, "His forest is now our forest! Our empire grows evermore . . . but do you think all we got was a bunch of fucking trees?" Slugger said with a smirk. He then whistled piercingly, and a pair of trucks full of guns and government-stamped ammunition crates rolled up ceremoniously. The crowd erupted even more, perversely aroused by the new sight.

"This is only the beginning, my friends." As Slugger continued, Shane and Bastian desperately looked for Carli through the bustling mob, and a fear for the worst began to rise within them. "There is still so much more for us to take. So much more for us to see . . . We will bring civilization back, in our image. We are on a course that will lead to an unstoppable legacy. A future that will call us the founding fathers." Slugger finished his speech and the crowd cheered once more before it was satisfied and dispersed.

Shane watched the leader and saw Moose whispering something into his ear. Moose then pointed to Shane and Bastian. Slugger looked over, nodded, and patted his gate captain on the back. Through the fading crowd, Bastian's gaze suddenly locked on a stupendous sight that he could not look away from: monsters of shell and teeth, tamed by the cruelty of fire and metal. He stared as a crew unfastened Homer and Marge from their reins with caution and an older man gently led them off.

The warlord approached the two newcomers with a wide smile as Ben's great shadow loomed over him from behind. "Shane and Bastian," he spoke. The two nodded, unsure of what to say. "Newbies, huh? Well, what do you think of this place so far?" he inquired.

"It's incredible," Shane stated.

"Are you just sucking my dick, or do you mean that?" Slugger tilted his head.

". . . No, it's great," Shane said with subtle resentment.

"I heard you were a history man, is that right?"

"That's right."

"Good, good. You don't mind if I talk to him first, do you?"

Slugger asked Bastian.

"No," Bastian said plainly.

"Awesome. Come on, professor," Slugger said kindly while Bastian watched him lead his friend away, as if fearing he would not see him again.

Slugger, followed by Big Ben, led Shane to his crooked tower. Once they entered, they took an immediate right down a hallway that opened up to a large room. It had four classical armchairs of the same set. They were made of aged hardwood, courted with lusty velvet fabric, and huddled next to a fireplace. A licking flame, like the warlord's tongue, was kept alive night and day. The room itself was filled with stocked bookcases, dusty old maps, and an enormous golden globe glinting at the center of it all, like the star of some important solar system.

Shane was delighted and almost couldn't believe his eyes. "I had more, but I've started to spread my collection . . . spread the knowledge, you know?" Slugger arrogantly walked about the room. "Please, have a seat," he said, gesturing to the chairs. The three of them sat down. Shane glanced at the goliath for a moment, and a sickening dread, like the giant's shadow, engulfed him. He could feel Ben staring back through his stringy bangs. "Just pretend he's not there. So, history man . . . what do you make of this world?" Slugger asked while propping his feet up on the coffee table in front of him.

". . . What do you mean?" Shane asked.

"I mean, as a man who has studied our past, did you expect this future?" Slugger explained.

Shane pondered the question for a moment. "I don't think anyone could have expected this. If you're talking about the end of civilization, well, if history has taught us anything, it's that society is the most fragile thing of all," he posited. Slugger nodded in agreement.

"Well said," he stated.

"That was a good speech out there," Shane offered.

Slugger smiled sinisterly. "Thank you. Care for a drink?"

"Maybe just water."

"Smart man," he said with approval as he got up to grab three glasses and a canteen of water from off a shelf. He poured the three of them a glass and sat back down. "You know . . . my Lost Boy's aren't usually so nice to strangers. What'd you guys do to get on their good side so quick?" Slugger inquired.

"They're good kids . . . and I realized their secret pretty fast," Shane stated simply.

Slugger looked at him for a moment and crushed his eyebrows downward.

"Hmm . . . and she let you live, huh? I'll trust her judgment. Talia is my future. She will rule one day with an iron fist, but the world is not ready for her yet," he stated smugly. "I assume that you are smart enough and beyond threats, but I feel like I just have to say this anyway. Any of my men find that out . . . I will kill you, as slowly as I possibly can," Slugger warned.

Shane studied the man's face before he responded. "Aren't you in control?" he inquired politely.

Slugger pricked up a quick smirk and thought for a while before speaking again.

"I think you'll appreciate this. I knew a great man once . . . a man I had to kill . . . and he told me a story. There were three brothers, and each ran their own respective tribes. They came together in times of war or trade, but began growing further and further apart. One year, a drought with no warning scorched the Earth. As is tradition, they each went out and led a party to seek water, game, and vegetation for their people . . . and one by one, each of their parties fell. The three brothers were all that remained. Interestingly enough, they all came across a strange oasis at precisely the same time. It was beautiful and promising. They hadn't seen each other in years, but they all knew what the others were there for.

"As they began to fight, a spirit exited the water, and her singing lulled and hushed them. She asked why they were there. The oldest spoke of the drought beyond the oasis and the trouble brought upon the land. She then told them of the cruel nature of the forgotten oasis, and that once their people stepped foot on the grass, the waters would dry up and the green, vanish. Knowing the secret truths of the world, she pitied mortal men, and so offered each a gift of their own choosing. The oldest asked for a cow that never died or felt pain, and healed its flesh overnight once taken, in order to feed his dwindling tribe. The middle son asked for a large barrel of water that never emptied or dirtied in order to sustain his thirsty people. But the youngest . . . he looked to his brothers, and then to the spirit. He knew he would be out searching again after some time, and there was no one gift that could provide his tribe all that they needed . . . until he realized, there was. He asked for a gun . . . a gun he could fire infinitely, and never need to reload."

Slugger beamed giddily. "He then shot his brothers dead and ended up with all three of the magic items. Ha! It's a great story really, but still . . ." he took in a deep breath, ". . . it is a little more complicated in execution. I now have the magical guns and ammo, I have eyes and claims on the lands beyond, but then what? Control is never absolute. I lead these men, I inspire them, I teach them . . . but I must understand them and the things I cannot change within them. Human nature is the most terrible beast of all."

Shane nodded in agreement and took a sip of water.

"It's nice talkin' like this. Wisdom is a rare commodity these days, but is that all you're bringing to the table?" Slugger calmly asked.

Shane hesitated for a moment, then responded confidently. ". . . With all due respect, despite this amazing place you've built, we did not come here to join you guys." Slugger's mood switched immediately, as if his pride had been sullied, and he cocked his head in confusion.

"Then why are you here?" he asked with rising annoyance.

"We were traveling, and we lost a friend . . . all signs pointed here," Shane said. Slugger scratched his forehead.

"What was his name?" he inquired.

"Her name was Carli," Shane answered sternly, and the name seemed to cause a ripple effect. Slugger's aura noticeably darkened, and he remained silent with a blank face for a few suspenseful moments. "Have you seen her?" Shane persisted. Slugger hesitated and glanced over at Ben, but received nothing. The madman then turned back to face Shane and slowly smiled.

"Yeah, we saw her," he said eerily. Shane suddenly stood up and clenched his fist. The giant next to him did the same. Slugger remained sitting with a sick smirk. "Woah, let me tell you the story first . . . I . . . uhh . . . filled her fucking face with bullets," he said coldly, ending with a deep cackle.

Shane swung his fist, but it was caught by the giant. Ben then grabbed hold of Shane's throat and lifted him in the air while he tried to kick the monster futilely. "You cared for her? Well, so did I. I knew her before all this. I knew who she really was . . . and I fucking killed her . . . and you won't be able to do a goddamn thing about it! You and your friend will want to kill me, ha! You know how many men and women have tried to kill me? I don't even know anymore . . . everybody wants a piece of me, 'cuz one way or another, I got a piece of them. So, due to your affiliation with her, you are hereby banished from paradise. No water, no food—except for what you came in with, of course. Remember, this is the start of civilization.

"Once we let you out of those gates, you really have only two options. You can plot to kill me, and we can play this mouse pretending he's a cat game until you give up and rot to death or . . . you can move on and go far away from here, spread that wisdom of yours. The second choice is the smart one, but I have a feeling you're going for the first. So, come and get me. I don't want to kill you . . . no . . . I want you to want to kill yourself, and then do it," he explained, maniacally lapping at the hungry dribble at his lips.

Shane passed out in the giant's grasp, swinging and kicking no more, and was then dropped to the floor. "I enjoyed our talk . . . brief as it was," Slugger said to no one as the flames of his passion were suddenly cooled.

Chapter XI – Below the Heavens

Shane woke up on his back, staring into dark skies while a full moon stared back at him with its purple gleam. A silver stripe streaked across the blackness before the trail of the shooting star faded. He was moving, and noticed he was being dragged along in a wheelbarrow. He sat up and saw Bastian pulling, and by his side, Vinny.

"What's going on?" Shane asked deliriously. They both stopped and turned around.

"Why didn't you tell me about your arm? You're probably going to die now," Bastian remarked, cold and resentful. Shane lay back down without a word.

"It's at least a few days walk. We gotta move through the night," Vinny stated.

When the morning approached, Vinny handed out cans of beans for breakfast. "What happened?" Shane asked while Bastian opened his can for him.

"You tell me. One moment everything's fine, and the next, they're pulling guns on me, dragged your unconscious body through the dirt, and threw us out; with our stuff at least. The leader said something to me before they shut the gates . . . he told me he'd be waiting, whatever the hell that means. This one followed me and told me about your arm. Guess we got no other choice but to trust him and take you to wherever he wants to go," Bastian exclaimed as he angrily opened his own can.

"He killed her," Shane's words cracked through his voice. Bastian remained silent. "And he wants us to try and kill him for it. It's all a fucking game to him, and I don't know if we can do this," Shane muttered hopelessly. He then looked over to Vinny, who was quietly distressed and sorrowful. "If this is some kind of trap, just kill us now, please," he added. Vinny did not respond and instead gazed meaningfully at his compass.

They walked day and night west, through wasteland and forest. The group traveled for over a week without any conversations or shared thoughts until they saw a beach and the great ocean on the horizon. The sand was black with sharp pillars of cloudy stone protruding from the ground. A large wrecked cruise ship split in two was beached ashore.

"Well, this is all the west we can go, so I'm guessing this is it," Bastian stated.

". . . Yeah" Vinny said, clearly unsure.

"You're gonna do all the talking, right?" Bastian inferred. Vinny nodded in response, focused on the beauty and calm of the water ahead. He led them over the line of hills covered in steel blue grass blades, and they found a small pond. Bastian dragged Shane around it. Vinny, however, tried to jump over. As he was in the air, a slimy tongue shot out from the water and wrapped around the man's ankle. Bastian let go of the wheelbarrow and dove for Vinny's hand. Shane fell out and remained too weak to get up. Bastian got a hold of Vinny and pulled him up with unnatural strength. As he dragged him away from the pond, the tongue refused to let go. A large eel-like creature with long antennas and hinged mandibles was ripped out of its lair, and Vinny took out his knife and sliced through the creature's tongue. The animal screeched in agony and slithered back into the deep.

"Thanks man," he said as Bastian helped him up. They both picked up Shane and plopped him back into the wheelbarrow.

"Don't move or we'll fucking shoot you!" a feminine voice rang out from the shadows. Nine women armed with rifles and handguns surrounded them with triggers ready. "Who the hell are you?" the grey-haired leader demanded.

"Friends," Vinny calmly stated with his hands up.

"We don't have any friends with balls," she said as her soldiers chuckled. Vinny made eye contact with a girl, bright with Japanese beauty, to his right.

"Emi . . . I had to come," Vinny said softly as he started to approach her. She rammed him in the stomach with the barrel of her rifle before he got close. Vinny coughed and retched and held his stomach in agony on the floor. ". . . I fuckin' hate you sometimes," he barely managed to get the words out.

His attacker couldn't hold in her laughter. "No, you don't," she said between giggles.

"How does he know your name?" the wrinkled leader demanded. Emi's grin was wiped off and she did not answer. Vinny stood up, eventually gathering his strength together.

"Where do you think you got all these weapons, huh?" he asked rhetorically. "We found each other on the open road. She was going to kill me, but she hesitated and some of the other men were incoming . . . so I promised her I'd direct them away if she gave me a chance, and she did," he said proudly. "Emi, please tell them."

"It was fun for a few months . . . but then I didn't see you any more after that, did I?" she remarked unappreciatively.

"My duties got redirected and I couldn't act suspiciously. Your safety was too important," he protested.

The leader scoffed. "Men are weak. Nothing but scared, hungry little animals. And what's wrong with this one?" she said, staring at Shane with a hawkish look.

"Take . . . take it off," Shane said before he passed out again. One of the women lifted his sleeve.

"It's been infected for a while," the woman stated.

"Please, save him," Bastian pleaded with swelling tear ducts.

"Why did you bring them?" Emi barked at Vinny.

"Because, they made me realize how important you are, even before they knew about you," he said softly. He then turned to face the rest. "Emi told me about you. What happened here. I promised her I would never bring that fate your way, and I won't. These men . . . they aren't like the others. They had a friend named Carli, and they traveled very far to find her, but when they did, she was already torn apart by the very men you equate us to," Vinny stated passionately.

The leader glanced over at Emi. "So, he just gave you these guns?" she asked, and Emi nodded. "We know about your group. Didn't know one of ours was fucking one of yours but . . . we still know more than you think. Still, if this is a trap, I must tell you it's not a very good one," she said as she strolled over to Shane. "Jesus . . . you guys can't even cauterize an amputation right." The leader remarked rudely as she analyzed the infection. She put her hand on his forehead. "He's burning up. I don't think he's going to make it," she said icily.

"Are you a doctor?" Bastian inquired with desperation.

"Yes, but . . . I still won't be able to do much."

"Let's take him to the shack and at least try," Emi suddenly interrupted.

The elderly woman took in a deep breath and shut her fathomless eyes. "Even the best of men have that weakness in them," she said grimly.

"Karen . . . what about Arthur? Are you saying he's no different?" Emi inquired.

"Yeah! Him too, but he doesn't have any fuckin' legs so, I think we'll be fine!" the leader of the group screamed at the girl.

"And he won't have an arm," Emi replied, keeping her cool. Karen stormed up to Emi, eyes boring into hers.

"What about the giant over there? What about your smooth talker, huh?" she berated the young woman.

"Carli!" Shane screamed. Everyone went silent, startled by the outburst.

". . . Shane?" Bastian asked, but there was no response. Shane was in a delirious state, drifting in and out of consciousness.

"Fine, bring him. But remember what I said." Karen led the group toward the beach. A beautiful woman with big blue eyes and a large dark afro, dressed in cargo pants and a tank top, walked up to the pond with a handmade fishing spear. She patiently aimed and chucked it into the water. She pulled the string it was attached to and dragged out the lifeless eel-like creature.

Once they arrived at the beach, the sun rested high in the sky, but they noticed heavy clouds inconsiderately soaking up most of the rays. Bastian and Vinny helped Shane onto a stretcher in the middle of a run-down beach shack. The shack had missing planks from the roofs and walls, broken windows, and was leaning slightly to the left, burrowing into the black sand. Inside was an array of unfamiliar plants separated into pots. Hanging from the ceiling were bright green trails of leaves that rolled up tightly, on their own, in reaction to the human presence. Karen examined Shane while Bastian and two guards observed.

"I honestly don't understand how he has survived this long," she said doubtfully. Suddenly, a supersonic detonation sent out shockwaves, miles high above the clouds. Everyone ran out in a panic to witness the commotion . . . all but Bastian, who remained by Shane's side. Vinny, Emi, Karen, and the rest of her group watched in awe as a colossal extraterrestrial mothership drenched in flames flew with high velocity down toward Earth. It crashed into the far-off waters. Moments later, an armada of alien ships appeared from the heavens.

www.ingramcontent.com/pod-product-compliance
Lightning Source LLC
Chambersburg PA
CBHW030618130626
46552CB00002B/626